MIRROR/MIRROR

Mirror/Mirror

A DRAMATIC STORY OF FATHER AND SON; TWO IMAGES CAUGHT IN A WEB OF SOCIETY, FRIENDSHIP, AND LOVE

Damion Peddie

Write My Wrongs, Co., United States
www.writemywrongsediting.com
Copyright © 1999 Damion A. Peddie

Reg. No. 30558-037

FOREWORD

What goes around comes around

To be aware of something that is unseen, you have to take pride in reality

INTRODUCTION: ABOUT THE AUTHOR OF MIRROR/MIRROR

Off the coast of sunny, tropical Jamaica, a white mansion stood on a hill, beautifully decorated with all sorts of fruit trees, flowers, and a wide array of green grass. A mansion fit for a king, it had seven bedrooms, five baths, an Olympic-sized pool and jacuzzi, an indoor sauna, tennis and basketball courts, and last but not least, a private man-made pond with all sorts of fish.

Damion sat on his veranda, overlooking the vast stretch of land he owned.

He sighed contently and admired what the joy of living was really about. A reminiscent thought flashed across his mind. He stared blatantly into the evening sun, then started to cry, the tears he shed coming from a place of great meaning and mixed feelings. He spoke to himself, asking how he'd made it thus far out of a dreadful system—the loss of friends, family, pain, guilt, and the lies.

Growing up, society had molded him. He was born in Jamaica, leaving at the age of seven to live in America.

Life there was a whole different ball game. He'd thought, at the time, it was the best place on earth; no uniform schooling, no praying before classes, and at the age of sixteen, school wasn't a must. To be black and divine, you simply had to follow the characteristics of men like Frederick Douglass, Booker T. Washington, Marcus Garvey, Malcolm X, and Bill Cosby.

He was brought up in the northwest area of Washington, D. C. His household consisted of himself, his mom, his stepfather, and four sisters. His schooling and upbringing were peachy until he was introduced to peer pressure! Peer pressure was his best friend, kicking self-esteem to the curb. From there, it was all over. After that, the only parents he obeyed were materialism and lust.

As the teenage years caught up with him, he remembered it as the roughest part of his life, complete with gang banging, robberies, and close calls with death. On his patio, he sat back and wondered: if he was dead, should people mourn for him?

Hell, no! Allah gave him the gift of life, love, and understanding. But, not knowing his divine purpose, he'd let the negative influences of society lead him astray.

He'd been in every penal system: Scared Straight, juvenile hall, state facilities, and prison. There, he'd learned more about himself than in society. Once incarcerated, the mind rid itself of all disease that society produced so one could focus on becoming better.

Think about it: how could he be better without the love of family? How could be better when the school didn't teach him the history of his people? How could he be better with "ghetto" surroundings? How could he be better if all he knew was a church, liquor store, strip tease bar, library, and drugs on the corner?

Which was he to choose from? The church told him to never question God, and He'd save him one day. The liquor store told him to drink a bottle of Wild Irish Rose, and he'd enjoy God. The strip club told him to give money, and he'd leave with a goddess. The library based its history on someone else's god. And the drugs were one of the only ways he knew how to survive.

Young, deaf, blind, and mentally dead—what was he supposed to do? He turned to his left, and on his table sat his books of encouragement: the Bible, the Koran, Holy Tablets, and history books of great black leaders. One man couldn't change a nation, so he'd start with his family. Look, listen, humble yourselves, and learn. We say Allah doesn't give you any more than you can bear; well, bear righteousness, bear responsibility, bear love for one another, and most importantly, bear self.

Damion shattered the glass that only showed a picture of failure. The pieces were those of a new beginning. Luckily, some knew when it was time to face their own revelation before participating in the folds of society.

Mirror/mirror on the wall, this story is about to tell it all.

CHAPTER ONE

On February 3, 1996, Christopher Canine sat awaiting death row at the Santa Pablo Federal Prison. He was scheduled to be put to death in six days' time.

Christopher Canine was not special, but he was a man, a human being with feelings and needs. Even at forty-eight years old, his six-foot-eight frame, dark and muscular, made him the worst nightmare of any son of a bitch who crossed his path.

It had been eighteen years since the cell doors slammed behind him, closing him off from the world he once knew. The sound had rung like the trapdoor on a gallows, where only the support of a chair held his balance as he waited to fall to the strangulation of the rope.

Although he wasn't special, he was a breed of man who'd learned to withstand the trials of imprisonment, salvaging his dignity and his sanity. But the cost was great. He'd earned a tormented soul; nightmares more terrible than some of his worst days played while he lay wide-awake on Earth's plane.

In his depression, he descended into a personal hell from which he never returned, one he was willing to share. Sleep often escaped him, and that morning was no exception.

At two-thirty a.m., he was awakened by the same terrible nightmares of the past—the murders, robberies, innocent bloodshed—events so horrible, even Christopher shook in his heavy prison boots. He sat up and summoned a guard in his usual manner.

"Hey, honky motherfucker! This is cell two-thirteen. Goddammit, hurry up, you white piece of shit."

Christopher heard the keys rattle, knowing the guard, in *his* usual manner, would probably drag his dead ass from the chair he'd sat in for the last eighteen years and challenge him with off-colored remarks.

"What do you want, punk? Why don't you get your ass to sleep?" the guard yelled from halfway down the cell block.

For Christopher, the response was automatic: "Open this motherfuckin' cage, and we'll see who's a punk."

The guard signaled to the cell monitoring station—he'd learned years ago to never be too careful with a death-row convict—and the monitor opened the door, allowing the guard to enter Christopher's cell block. As he approached cell 213, he saw Christopher doing sit-ups, sweating like hell.

"That won't do you any good." The guard laughed. "Electric volts ain't scared of no goddamn muscle."

"Fuck you, you illiterate white motherfucker! Get me the chaplain, now!"

"Are you crazy, boy? It's two-thirty-something in the morning. The chaplain ain't coming to see your punk ass at this time of day, so lie down!"

Before responding, Chris did his last sit-up, sweat pouring from his face. He looked up at the guard, his heart visibly beating through his sweaty chest, then growled, "Listen, cocksucker, you want me to tell the warden? It's my right to summon the chaplain anytime I want."

The guard leaned on the bars of Chris's cell, his keys knocking against the raw steel, the sound ringing into Chris's mind. After a moment of silence, the guard snorted.

"That's your right, alright." He laughed, then walked back down the hall, his mockery echoing off the bare walls. "It'll be your last, too."

Sitting on his bed with his face in his hands, Chris's thoughts drifted to memories of how he'd met the chaplain.

***

The night he'd arrived at Santa Pablo, Chris sat in a small truck, similar to a Brink's Bank van, heavily guarded by two regular cars following behind. He wondered why they needed the entourage. All he'd done was kill an inmate in a maximum-security federal prison. He smiled, leaned his head back, and closed his eyes.

The vehicle came to a stop in front of a huge metal gate, seventy, maybe seventy-five feet tall, with spikes on top. It was the door to "The Devil's Playhouse," as the inmates at the other prisons referred to it. While the gate was gray, the spikes on top were turning rusty after years of battering by Mother Nature's crazy weather.

It was hailing, but Chris couldn't tell as the gate opened, making a screeching sound, overwhelming even the thunderstorm. It reminded him of a horror film.

As the vehicles entered, they went down a slope, heading for a basement-like corridor, which connected to a ramp taking them even further down. They drove at least four or five more flights before coming to a halt. The truck then backed up to a door that swung open, revealing four gentlemen: two in uniform, one in civilian dress, and the last an older guy with a receding hairline who looked about fifty-five years old. He wore fine-rimmed spectacles, and anyone could tell he was a priest or chaplain from their first look, given his all-black clothing with the little white collar.

The two uniformed guards, each about six feet tall, walked toward the truck and opened the back doors. Inside, Chris sat in the same position, smiling, his eyes closed. One of the guards grabbed him by the arm and ripped him out of the back, pulling so hard Chris missed his step and tripped. Both guards picked him up, one holding each shoulder as he regained his balance.

Once Chris was righted, the gentleman in the expensive suit walked up to him and looked him straight in the eye. The two devilish faces differed on a subtle level: one a cold-blooded killer, the other a patient murderer.

To break the stare down, the chaplain put his hand on Christopher's shoulder, addressing him. "How are you, my son? Welcome. I'm Chaplain Rogers. If you need me, you may summon me any time, day or night."

"And I'm Warden Hogg." The man in the suit cut the chaplain off. "Have a pleasant stay." He sneered before walking away.

The chaplain placed a small Bible in Chris's pocket before nodding to the uniformed guard to take him away. A few feet down the hall, Chris stopped and looked back at the chaplain as if he wanted to tell him something, but instead, he turned away slowly and kept walking down the dark, cave-like hallway.

***

A loud buzzing came over Chris's intercom, startling him from his memories. He nearly jumped out of his skin as the loudspeaker shrieked to life above his head.

"The chaplain will be in to see you shortly."

About thirty minutes later, the chaplain stood in front of the monitoring station. The guard, who'd never left his chair, got up and sighed.

"Right this way, sir. The guy in two-thirteen wanted to see you. Don't know what about."

The chaplain, in his usual humble manner, nodded to the guard. "Show me to his cell."

As the guard led the chaplain down the cold, damp hallway to Chris's cell block, Chaplain Rogers felt the ghostly stillness of death roaming through the halls. Cells surrounded him on both sides, filled with human beings awaiting their day of death. He saw the fear in their eyes, a few of them coming to the bars and staring as Rogers walked by.

As he approached Chris's cell, he greeted the inmate. "In the name of the Father, the Son, and the Holy Ghost, I am here to give you guidance, my son. What is it I can help you with?"

The guard butted in: "Do you need a chair?" He gestured to the one across from Chris's cell.

Rogers nodded as Chris walked forward and sat down, facing him.

After looking into the chaplain's eyes, deciding whether or not he should spill his guts to the stranger, he began.

"Father, I haven't always been like this. It's by force, not by choice."

The guard passed the chair to the chaplain to sit on, then returned to his post. Sitting contently, Rogers focused on what Chris was saying.

"Well, son, if you need to get something off your chest, I'm here to listen."

At that moment, Chris felt much better. He'd reached an understanding with the gentleman in front of him. And so, he began his story.

"Me, my brother, my sister, and my mom moved up to Washington D.C. from South Carolina. We didn't have a father figure around. Mom said he ran off after losing his job. I guess he couldn't handle feeding three hungry little mouths, but Mom got a job offer that paid decent money and better benefits.

Back then, it was hard for a black woman to get a job in the South with all the racism still hanging in the air, so she decided to move up North. There was less prejudice as far as blacks were concerned. At that time, I was nine, my sister, Carol, was twelve, and my brother, Pete, was fifteen years old."

The chaplain interrupted to ask, "How was your relationship with your family?"

"Well, we were very close."

Chris continued telling his life story to the chaplain:

Pete was short, heavyset, and took after our father. He was kinda like the man of the house. I loved him so much. The only problem was he always did everything the right way.

Carol was the total opposite. That's probably why me and her stuck together like glue. We were the closest in the whole family. Carol was very pretty—looked a lot like our mom when she was younger. She had long, shiny black hair, and her skin was a lot like mine. She always looked older than she was, and no matter how much she ate, she always had a slim figure.

My mom was an older version of Carol, and I loved her, too. She was a strong woman, and no matter what, she tried her best not to let us see an unhappy day.

One Sunday afternoon, after church let out, everyone gathered outside on the steps. Me and Carol were the last of our family to come out, and we met up with our mom and Pete, who were talking to the preacher. We ran up to Mom and started begging her to walk home that day. Well, Mom turned and looked at us, and we figured she was in a good mood because she nodded yes. Before she said anything else, we took off running. All we could hear was, "Watch both ways before crossing the street!"

It always seemed funny to me how we took the church bus home or got rides from some of Mom's friends each week. I never understood why, seeing as we only lived five blocks from our church.

Well, that day, me and Carol planned on stopping at the candy store to buy these new race cars and an African doll that she wanted. We saved up all month waiting on that day, and after crossing the street, we ran toward the store. But before we could get in the door, we encountered these six guys. Three were white, and three were black. It was strange to us because it was rare, seeing blacks and whites together in our neighborhood.

Coming out the door, they looked like something from a Fat Albert cartoon. I grabbed my sister's arm and pulled her close to me. But, of course, they stopped to look at us.

The tallest one out the bunch was a white guy, about five-foot-seven, maybe six feet. I remember he had this sandy-blond hair, devilish blue eyes, and a scar on the left side of his face. He spoke up and said, "Hey boys, check this out! The new kids on the block are coming from church."

Carol responded without thinking. She said something like, "That's right! You should be there, too!"

Then he snapped back at her, "Shut up, bitch! Don't tell me what to do."

So I stepped up to him and said, "Hey, punk! Don't be calling my sister no bitch."

Well, then the guy pulled out a knife and stuck it to my throat, put his hand on Carol's ass, and rubbed it while his buddies stood there and laughed like it was the funniest thing in the world.

I was upset, but I couldn't do anything, not with that knife at my throat. The very next words out of his mouth were, "See, motherfucker, I don't want you around here, get it?"

One of his buddies butted in and said, "Take your punk ass on home before he cuts your face off!" And after a moment, the others joined in and started chanting, "Yeah, Duke! Cut his face off!"

It felt like my whole world was ending, but I stood there facing him, not flinching, and told myself if I showed any type of weakness, they'd probably whip my ass right in front of my sister. Eventually, he pulled the knife away from my face, walked across the street, and sat on an old car, and the other five followed him.

After our dilemma, Carol and I didn't bother going into the store to get what we wanted. We headed straight home. I did look back to see if any of those guys were following us and noticed they all had brown paper bags in their hands with bottles inside.

We were almost home before I noticed Carol crying. I looked at her, then back at the guys on the old car, and I knew right then I had to pay those guys back for humiliating my sister.

Years later, I ran into one of Duke's old buddies. He didn't remember me until I brought up the argument, and he told me that night after Carol and I left, Duke and the other guys were still hanging out by the store, still sitting on that old car. Duke's buddy Skip—a short, chubby guy, around two-hundred and fifty pounds with cropped blond hair, blue eyes, always kept some kind of food in his mouth like some kind of pig, you couldn't miss him—he said, "Hey, Duke, how long before you get that new pussy?"

Duke had the gall to tell him, "That's church pussy. It'll be a little longer than the regular."

That's when a third guy from the group joined in the conversation. He was one of the black guys named Sly.

Apparently, he and Duke grew up together. His father worked for Duke's family at the hardware store. He was a little shorter than Duke, well-built with a jet-black complexion, beady brown eyes, and slick black hair. He reminded me of a broke pimp. He piped up and said, "You think she's a virgin?"

And Duke was like, "Yeah, man. Most of them Southern bitches are virgins."

Well, that's when Sly saw me heading their way, jumped off the hood of the car, and pointed up the road, saying, "Look who's coming! It's that little punk!"

"So." Skip giggled and tried to look all menacing-like. "I guess the little nigger wants his ass-whipping now."

Now, a couple hours before encountering Duke and his boys the second time, I told my mom and sister I was going to buy some ice cream. My sister wanted to go too, but I told her I wouldn't be long. She knew I was up to something because I never went anywhere without her, so I hurried off down the street before she persuaded me to let her come.

I got to the corner, just out of sight, then made a U-turn and went right into this alley that led back to the rear of our house. I took one of Pete's baseball bats, wrapped it in a brown plastic garbage bag, and took that with me.

As I approached the six of them, one jumped off the car and pointed up the street. I couldn't make out what he said at that point because my heart was pounding so hard in my ears. But I walked up to them and pulled out the bat so fast, not one of those guys could stop me. I started hitting Duke over the head and face, and all his friends did was run.

I didn't stop until I saw his brains splattered all over my bat and the street.

CHAPTER TWO

February 3, 1996, around seven-thirty a.m., it was a cool Saturday morning in the northwest part of Washington, D.C. Eighteen-year-old Steve Canine stood about five-foot-eight, his dark complexion and muscular build making him look older than his age. He seemed to dwarf his mother Lyn—a beautiful, slim woman with a light complexion—even if he only stood a couple of inches taller than her. They lived together in a quiet neighborhood.

Lyn owned two daycare centers located not far from her house. Even so, she spent a lot of her time at home taking care of and keeping a watchful eye over her only son, who seemed to grow up a bit too fast for her liking.

That particular morning, the house was quiet everywhere except Steve's bedroom. He opted to occupy his time by having sex. The lovemaking must have been intense because Steve had her groaning so loud that the only way to cut the noise down was to put a pillow over her face. Her screams even overrode the radio as it played on full blast. After a few more minutes of humping and grinding, the moaning stopped with Suzie shivering in Steve's arms. Sweating like hell after the exertion, Steve grabbed a towel and wiped her face.

"Damn, Suzie," he said, looking her dead in the eyes, "you've got the best pussy I've had in years."

"Don't say that," she groaned. "You'll make me feel like a whore."

"Why not?" Steve rolled over to his side of the bed. "It's the truth! Why would I lie about good pussy?"

"Boy, shut up." She hit him with a pillow, then rolled over on her elbow. "So, what are we going to do today?"

"Well, you're gonna take your ass home."

"So that's it, huh?" Suzie sat up with a frown on her face, folding her arms. "Fuck me, then dump me?"

"No, baby," Steve said as he pulled her back on top of him and kissed her, "but you know I've got things to do."

Suzie knew there was only one more thing she could do to try and persuade him to let her stay. She ducked under the covers and played with his john.

He lay there for a moment, enjoying the feeling, but jumped up before Suzie started something he had no control over. He didn't bother looking back at her while he went straight to his closet and took out a box. He emptied it onto the bed, and a Ziploc bag filled with rocked-up cocaine tumbled out.

Seeing its contents, Suzie knew she couldn't persuade him, so she pouted and sighed. "Don't you take any days off with that shit?"

"It's not shit. And I get a day off when the police lock me up."

***

Corey, a close friend of Steve's, lived fifteen blocks from his house, just off the main avenue in the busiest part of the neighborhood. The eighteen-year-old lived with his mother, Pearl.

Pearl was about six feet tall with a caramel-brown complexion and long black hair, not to mention a slim waist for her forties. Unfortunately, after she got on welfare, all Pearl did was sit in the house, collect her monthly check, and smoke crack cocaine.

Corey knew about his mother's habit and had been fighting a losing battle. Every time he tried to get her into rehab, she argued, saying she wasn't an addict. So, instead of having her go out and buy from people—especially his boys on the corner—he just gave it to her.

About the same time Steve was fooling around with Suzie, Corey quickly jumped out of bed and ran to the bathroom. He stuck his hand behind the toilet, feeling for something. When he didn't find it, he slammed his hand on top of the bowl. He took a few seconds, thinking, before he sprinted directly to his mother's room.

As he opened her door, a cloud of smoke greeted him. From the smell, he knew it wasn't tobacco.

His nose adjusted, and he saw his mother sitting on the edge of the bed with a piece of mirror, a razor blade, some cigarettes, and a beer can bent in the middle with ashes and a piece of cocaine perched on top. She didn't notice him standing there until she held the can up to her mouth to inhale the smoke wafting out.

Corey had no doubt that the drugs he was looking for so desperately had all gone up in smoke.

All Pearl could say for herself when she saw him was, "You told me I could have as much as I want." Her eyes were wide open, and she was slurring as she spoke.

"But the whole bag, Mom?" Corey gestured at what little was left. "The shit's not even paid for yet."

Pearl saw her son's anger and replied, "If you want, I can sell the TV."

Standing there, shoulders slumped, he answered, "It's okay. I'll find a way," then walked out and closed her door. He looked up at the ceiling and mumbled, "I've got to get her some help."

He heard the phone ringing and ran downstairs to answer it. On the other end of the line was his buddy Pee-Wee. Standing about five-foot-five, the seventeen-year-old thought all the girls adored him because of his curly hair, though his handsome face and well-built body didn't hurt.

"What's up, niggah? I got some juicy news, and this shit is the bomb!"

"If it ain't about me getting some money, it ain't the bomb," Corey replied.

Pee-Wee, happy on the other end, didn't know about Corey's mood.

"Fuck money! It's about pussy, and lots of it."

"You need lots of money to get lots of pussy."

Pee-Wee was persistent in his attempts to get his friend to go with him. "Not this time! All we need is some weed, and the party's on!"

After hearing that, Corey gave in. If he had to be broke, the next best thing was to get high and fuck for free.

Pee-Wee yelled into the phone again. "You remember Pepsi and Paula? Them hoes are fucking for weed, man, and what's better—check this out—they live with some other freaks, and some of them are dykes."

"So all we need is some weed, and we fuck everybody?"

"That's right!" yelled Pee-Wee. "Well, maybe not everybody. The dykes might not want to give up the pussy."

"Fuck it!" Corey answered, sounding more cheerful. "We'll just have our own freak show and get some pussy."

However, even while talking to Pee-Wee, everything going through Corey's mind was about money and the best way to get his mother into rehab.

He must have fallen silent for too long because Pee-Wee yelled at him again, "Are you listening, niggah?"

"Yeah, I heard you… Just thinking if you keep going in raw, you won't have a life to fuck with."

Pee-Wee didn't respond.

Corey still didn't believe it could be so easy, so he asked again, "Are you sure we don't need any money?"

"You can bring money if you want to be Santa," Pee-Wee replied, "but all I'm giving is plenty of dick and some smoke."

Corey laughed. In spite of his misgivings, he knew his buddy wouldn't lie to him.

"Alright, let's do this. You gotta come get me, though. My car's in the shop."

"I can't," Pee-Wee explained. "My mom has mine. So what? Just get dressed and meet me on the block. They'll be calling me around twelve."

Before hanging up his phone, Corey yelled, "Go to hell, niggah," into the receiver.

Pee-Wee yelled right back, "Alright, motherfucker!"

The only response was the dial tone in Pee-Wee's ear.

***

The rich, upscale neighborhood of Washington, D.C.—located across from Rock Creek Park and famous for the beautiful sights that ran from Maryland to Virginia—was populated with important people: senators, movie stars, businessmen, the works.

In that particular area, on the corner of Allison and Maple Nut Street, a large blue-and-white house sat on a hill facing the beautiful scenery of the park. It belonged to Sergeant

Ann-Marie Johnson and her husband, Jacob, who shared it with a live-in maid and two German Shepherds.

Ann-Marie had been a D.C. police officer for about five years. To the thugs, junkies, pushers, and her fellow officers, she'd acquired the nickname "Blondie," as she resembled the *Baywatch* star Pamela Anderson. Jacob, something of a yuppie type, owned his own business.

That morning, the sun shone directly into their kitchen, putting everyone in a happy mood.

"Good morning, love birds," said Elaine, the maid, walking over to the table where Blondie and Jacob were having a pot of coffee and some croissants.

Elaine had been with the Johnsons for about eight months after being recommended by her aunt, who was too sick to keep working for them. Even though Elaine was about thirty years old, the five-foot-four Puerto Rican's long black hair and plump figure gave her a more youthful appearance.

"Beautiful, isn't it?" Jacob replied.

Blondie sat directly across from Jacob reading the style section of *The Washington Post*. Between the drumming of his fingertips on the table, his furtive glances, and his soft throat clearing, she knew it was going to be one of *those* mornings.

Jacob had been trying to convince her to leave the street and work at the station ever since a spree of cop killings began in her district. Whenever he felt the urge rising, he started getting fidgety and uncomfortable, and all of the signs that particular morning pointed to conflict.

He folded his paper, setting it aside on the table.

"You know, I really think you should get a position at the station, honey. You don't fit in on the field."

Blondie didn't react to his statement. She was aware of how Jacob felt about her work. Jacob knew she was ignoring him, so he kept talking.

"The number of cop killings I've been reading about has gone up."

Blondie slammed down her paper on the table and let out a low sigh, as if to say, *Here we go again.* "Do I tell you how to do your job?"

"I don't have a position, honey." Jacob smirked. "I own my own business."

"So why don't you mind it?"

Even the smart remark didn't stop Jacob from pestering. He held up his cup for Elaine to fill with coffee, then said, "Honey, I'm just worried about you. That's all."

"Well, don't," Blondie snapped. "I like my job and love my position."

"Yeah?" Blondie's quip angered Jacob. Yelling from across the table, he retorted, "When your ass gets shot or killed, don't say I didn't warn you!"

Blondie grabbed the pot of coffee from Elaine's hands and threw it in his lap, spitting out a raging, "Fuck you, Jacob!" She grabbed her coat and hat, storming out of the house and slamming the door behind her.

Jacob sat in shock. He'd never seen Blondie so upset.

Out in front of the house, Blondie eagerly scrambled to get into her car. Her keys fell, and as she bent down to pick them up, she heard something moving in the bushes behind her. Normally, she would've checked it out, but it wasn't one of those days. Instead, she got into her car and drove off. The movement behind the bushes continued, and a figure appeared, machine gun in hand. The person was wearing an all-black ski suit and a mask with evil little eyes peering through, a scar cutting across the left one. They looked both ways, then ran off into the woods behind Blondie's house.

***

Upstairs, Jacob changed clothes in his bedroom, standing in front of his closet. He still couldn't get over his wife's outburst.

A pair of hands startled him out of his thoughts. Wrapping around his chest, they traveled down to his boxer shorts and began playing with his penis. He smiled as a familiar voice eased into his ear.

"Maybe I can take some tension off, if you'll let me."

Jacob slowly turned around, coming face-to-face with Elaine, who stood naked in front of him.

Jacob led her to the bed, and she lay across it, spread-eagle, beckoning him with her index finger.

As he crawled on top of her, he whispered in her ear, "You think she forgot something?"

"Don't worry," Elaine replied, "this won't take long."

He smiled, then buried his face into her soft breasts.

***

"I'm getting out of this marriage. It's not working out like I thought it was supposed to," Blondie said to herself.

Before Blondie could finish her thought, she stomped on her brakes to avoid blazing through the red light only a couple of blocks from the station where she worked.

The station was located on the corner of Georgia Avenue and Preston Street. A huge building painted blue and white, the station's rear radio tower dwarfed the buildings around it.

She parked her car, got out, and walked into the building, entering the elevator.

The station was the same every day: people making statements and police walking back and forth with either papers in their hands or someone in handcuffs. A few fellow officers greeted her, but she wasn't in the mood to reply, so she gave them a nod or a smile instead.

Approaching her desk, she saw a note stuck on her phone.

Come to my office A.S.A.P. —Lt.

She threw her coat on the desk and walked in the direction of the lieutenant's office.

Blondie felt ill at ease. She knew she hadn't been herself lately, with the death of her partner still on her mind. Along with her husband nagging her about the dangers of her job, it had been difficult to work the last few days.

The bold letters emblazoned with *Frederick Jones* shined on the lieutenant's door. A tall, broad-shouldered black man with short, graying hair, he was about fifty-five years old. He'd been a runner back in college, but after his accident, he left school and joined the police academy, working in the field ever since.

He turned around in his chair as Blondie walked in, greeting her with a smile, which told her the meeting wasn't about her performance.

"Hello, Blondie. Thanks for coming up so fast."

"What do you want, Lieutenant?"

"Eager as always." Jones chuckled. "But if you insist, please sit down."

Blondie narrowed her eyes, studying his unwavering smile before doing as he suggested.

"Alright. Now, what do you want?"

"Well, Sergeant Johnson." He took a deep breath. "I called you up to inform you that you're getting a new partner, starting today. His name is Patterson."

Blondie had known his smile was too good to be true.

"Hold it, Lieutenant. I don't need a babysitter. I can handle myself out there."

Jones leaned forward with both hands clasped as if praying, both elbows on his desk. He looked Blondie straight in the eyes with sympathy, then said, "I know you can. That's why I want you to look after him. He's a bit crazy."

She knew that the lieutenant had something up his sleeve, so she played along.

"So," she commented, "where's this Patterson?"

"He'll be here in a minute." He paused, inspecting Blondie closely before continuing. "So tell me, what's up in your part of town?"

Blondie wondered idly if her deadbeat husband was in on the scheme somehow. She knew, though, that she wasn't up on her neighborhood, so the lieutenant might've thought she couldn't run her area, which explained why he'd try to give her a partner.

After waves of thoughts ran through her mind, she finally answered, "Well, so far we haven't been able to find Kevin. But the drug selling is spreading on the hill and by the shopping mall. We have word that some guy named Big Dre is doing the supplying."

"Do we have any evidence to nail him?"

"Not yet, but soon. We have pictures of him as well as an informant who's working for us."

"Oh." Jones looked up to the door, cutting her off. "Here comes Patterson now."

Blondie turned around in her chair, her eyes settling upon a handsome man. Tall and blond with broad shoulders, he wore a sport jacket with a T-shirt underneath and a pair of fitted jeans that made his legs look as if he'd been riding a horse all his life.

She looked him over before finally introducing herself.

"Blondie's the name," she said, voice coming off cold and clipped as she fought her irritation with the lieutenant.

"Nice to meet you," Peterson replied, his voice warm, friendly, and unwavering.

Jones sat back in his chair, observing the two. *This*, he thought to himself, *is a perfect match.* He interrupted the staredown with a wave of his hand. "Okay, enough. Take Patterson on a sightseeing trip. I know he'll be interested."

Blondie got up and left, but before storming out of the office, she looked over at her new partner and said, "You think you can keep up?"

Jones stretched back in his chair, put his feet on his desk, then nodded to Patterson. "Welcome aboard."

Patterson smiled and walked out of the office.

He ran outside to catch up with Blondie, who was already in her car, backing up and ready to pull off. He jogged over and knocked on the window. She finally stopped when he wouldn't let go of the door but sped off before he closed it completely.

CHAPTER THREE

The morning was getting brighter, verging on noon. Steve was up and about. He got rid of Suzie, sending her downstairs to the living room while he figured out what to wear.

He picked up his gun and put it in the inside pocket of the jacket that was lying on the bed with all the other clothes. He picked out a black Versace sweater, a pair of black Guess jeans, and some black Timberland three-quarter cut boots. Since it would be cold later, he thought black would be the right color. Plus, it was perfect with his leather jacket. After putting everything on, he checked himself out in the mirror. The view was good.

His next task was to make it out of the house before his mom left her at-home office and saw him leaving with a girl. As he closed the door behind him, he made it to the second step before—

"Steve, get in here!"

He made a U-turn and headed for her room.

Lyn was kneeling down, unwrapping the vacuum, and getting ready to plug it in when he entered the room.

She looked up and commented, "What did I tell you about having these young girls spending the night?"

"The girl is not young. She just looks young."

"I don't care if she is young or looks young. You shouldn't have her here in the first place," Lyn snapped back.

Steve watched his mother trying to fix something on the vacuum. Seeing her frustration, he walked over to help her.

"Why can't they come over?" he asked. "If I sleep out, you argue. If I bring someone home, you argue."

"I'm not arguing," Lyn joked. "All I'm saying is you should just have *one*. Every time I look up, it's someone else."

Steve smiled as he tried to get the vacuum to work. After a minute, he got up and sat on the bed, gently moving a bunch of coupons to the side.

"Mom, if you're worried about me catching AIDS, no sweat. I always wear a condom."

"That's nice to know, but I'd still prefer one girl," answered Lyn.

Steve smiled at his mom. It was good to know that they could communicate about anything. "If I'm all the girls' choice, what can I say?"

Lyn stopped what she was doing and walked across the room. She touched his face with her small, gentle hands.

"You remind me so much of your dad. Just be careful." She gave him a big hug.

"Why don't you talk much about my father?" he whispered.

The question struck her with surprise, but she knew it was coming. The last time Steve had asked about his father was at his seventh birthday party. Since he was all grown up, she figured he needed a story.

But Lyn, stepping back and seeing a concerned look on her son's face, blurted out, "Some things are not good to discuss until the right time."

"I'm old enough, Mom. I can understand anything."

Lyn was about to say more but was interrupted by the ringing of the telephone.

Steve jumped up and ran downstairs to answer it. He picked up the receiver and waved his hand to tell Suzie to move over, plopping down on the couch.

"Hello?"

"What's up, youngin'?" asked Steve's buddy Corey. "Come and get me. My car's in the shop."

Steve heard what Corey said, but his lips were stuck to Suzie's. With one hand holding the phone and the other one steadily exploring the hot spot between his visitor's legs, he had to take time out for a breather to answer. "Not right now, I hope. I'm in the middle of something, and then I've got to drop Suzie off at home."

"So what? I'll ride with you. I'm bored and ain't doing shit!"

Suzie was getting Steve's hormones going again. He knew she almost had him. The only way out was—

"I'll stop by in a few minutes. Get ready."

Suzie knew she'd lost the battle again. Upset, she got up and walked over to the door.

It's a waste to get rid of some good pussy, he thought, then smiled. He had more important things to do that day.

Two cars were parked out in front of the house. One was his mom's sky blue 325i BMW. The other was his charcoal gray four-door Q45 Infiniti. Steve loved his car, with its tinted windows and loud stereo system. He thought his mother still believed the story of how he got it. He'd told her he won it playing dice. Just his lucky day. He had his friends corroborate by talking about the event all week. He knew his mom would buy it, but for how long?

As he opened the door for Suzie, he looked back at the house and saw his mom looking at him through her window. He waved at her, walked around to the driver's side, got in, and drove off.

***

It was six a.m. when the chaplain looked at his watch. It didn't look much different, other than the time—the face was still dark and musty. The light hanging over Christopher's cell was dull, like all the other lights that weren't broken or burnt out.

A guard walked by and tossed a peanut butter sandwich in Chris's cell without looking or saying anything.

The chaplain looked at his watch again. Six-fifteen. He looked at Christopher. The young man paced, his shadow following him like a dark secret. The chaplain looked around the cell and down the never-ending hallway of inmates. He knew it was hell down there. Screams popped through the air like fireworks, and every few seconds, guilt-stricken confessions twisted Roger's stomach as they revealed the horrors those men had committed in their free lives.

Chris stopped in the far corner of his cell and turned around. He wondered if the chaplain was paying any attention to his story.

The chaplain, sensing something in his quietness, said, "Chris, my son, please continue. Was your dilemma a major setback in your life?"

"Yes, chaplain. It took away nine years of my life by putting me behind bars. My mom fainted in the courtroom after the judge passed the ruling, and I experienced a lot of unpleasant things."

"Do you mind sharing some of those, or would you rather continue the story?" the chaplain asked.

Chris sat down on his bed, rubbed both hands together, and stared directly at the chaplain with bloodshot eyes.

Chris continued with his tale:

From the first day I set foot in the juvenile center, it was hell for me physically and mentally.

I was initiated with a beatdown in the shower by eight guys. Everyone did different things to me, like slapping a soaped-up wash cloth in my face, grabbing my butt cheeks, and hitting me in the stomach and chest, to name a few.

As the years went by, I saw things done to other boys that were far scarier than what happened to me. Honestly, my conviction and charge saved me because it kept 'em away. Most boys were raped, and some hung themselves because they couldn't stand it.

Every night, as I lay in my room, I couldn't get over the memory of what I'd done, so nightmares came frequently. The only thing that kept me going was the love of my family. Especially Carol. She wrote me every day.

Finally, my release day came. I was scared to leave, but happy to get out.

My family picked me up at the receiving home. Before I went out to meet them, I took a peek through the window to see how my family looked since I hadn't seen them in nine years.

My mother had gotten older, slight wrinkles forming around the eyes, but she was still beautiful. My sister had gotten taller, but she kept her girlish features. And my older brother, Pete, had turned into a pastor. From the look of it, he was serious, with his all-black suit and white neck piece. He had a bigger body frame than he used to, broad shoulders, and a gut like he'd been eating all the offerings he received.

The counselor called for me to come downstairs. As I came to the door, my sister was first to give me a giant hug, and my mother and brother came right behind her. I was overjoyed with the radiance of love I felt from my family. A few minutes later, my mother signed some paperwork, and we were on our way home.

I saw new buildings, shops, and stores. Everyone was taking turns filling me in. It was great. After what seemed like an hour—even if it was only about thirty minutes—we stopped at a fast-food deli and got some Chinese chicken fried rice and Mumbo sauce.

It was fun to be home. The old house wasn't much different, except for the color change and some flowers planted along the walk. The large wooden couch-like bench was still placed on the right. As I walked up to the porch, I noticed some tape around the legs and on the back, which told me it had been through hell.

But when I looked through the door, it was a whole different scene: new furniture and paintings. The only thing in its original place was the family portrait hanging on the wall next to a picture of Jesus.

I looked around for a minute, then headed back out the door to sit on the porch. Everyone looked at me like I was crazy. I told them I still felt kinda closed in and needed some air.

I tried to be part of coming home, but it was hard. Nine years is really a lot of time to be taken out of one's life.

A car drove past with teenagers hanging out the windows screaming, "Fuck the police!" The driver seemed to be the youngest of the bunch. He was propped up so close to the steering wheel that I thought he was going to go through the windshield.

A few minutes later, my sister came busting through the door with food in her hand and mouth, finally swallowing her bite to tell me, "That's what the neighborhood has gone to."

"They're just funning, that's all."

"What's the deal? Are you gonna sit out here all day? You're out now. Lighten up."

"I'm out, but it's more than that. You have to be in to understand. It smells different; there's new noise and real females! Not the ones in books or on TV. All we're used to is a faggot running around, trying to distract you."

Then Carol sat down beside me and said, "Speaking of females, I've got a couple of friends dying to meet you. I've told them so much."

I laughed and told her she couldn't've told them too much. I was still a goddamn virgin, after all.

"That's why I hooked you up with Cherry," Carol told me. "She's down to earth, plus she knows all about you."

"Bet she heard it straight from the horse's mouth."

"What! Are you calling your sister a horse?"

"Enough about horses! What have you been up to? Got anybody special in your life?"

Carol hugged me as if she were trying to put me in a chokehold. She smiled and said, "Don't play dumb. I told you about Reggie in my letters."

"I know, but you get 'em and drop them so much I thought…"

Carol put her finger on my lips and shook her head.

"You thought wrong because this one is different. He's the perfect man for me."

"Yeah, I'll have to check him out first."

"Don't bother. Mom and Pete like him a lot."

"So? Their checking and mine are totally different."

"Well, tell you what. He's coming by at seven. Then he's all yours."

Seemed like she liked him a lot.

***

Steve sat at the stoplight a block from his house. He was busy attending to his CD player, trying to find a suitable song to listen to while Suzie rested motionless in her seat. She couldn't think of anything else to keep Steve in the house. Her silence told him she was upset, so he decided to taunt her, blasting the music and bolting off as the light changed to green.

He used the back roads, an important rule in a big city filled with gangsters. With the life he lived, anything could happen. Someone could sneak up on him, an enemy might take a shot at him, or maybe an old girlfriend might see him and Suzie and decide to show her attitude. Even with his gun, he was vulnerable.

That was the life of a gangbanging drug dealer.

He took Third Street all the way up until it connected to New Hampshire Avenue. The avenue was quiet. On one side of the street were blocks and blocks of three- and four-story apartment buildings. On the other side was a wall protecting a large cemetery that stretched endlessly both in width and length. It was pretty safe to drive there, always quiet and lonely. It would be easy to observe another car a mile away if it were following behind.

Steve took a left on Allison Street, then another right on Second Street. He turned down his music and reduced his speed as he passed a row of houses, which all looked alike except for their color. With their small front yards, sixties-style wood porches, and screen doors, each with a bell hanging over it, they stood like a group of birds on a wire.

Steve stopped in front of the worst-looking one on the block. The yard was filled with leaves, the paint on the house was cracking up, and the wood on the banister of the porch looked like something out of a horror movie. Suzie glanced up at the house as the car stopped, then slumped back in her seat.

Steve blew his horn twice. A second later, Corey came running out with one hand keeping his pants from falling off and the other holding a sweatshirt and his belt. Steve stretched across the back seat to open the door for him.

Before getting in, Corey looked at Suzie sitting in the front, then threw his shirt and belt in the back, pulled up his pants, and stepped in.

"How come you're just putting on your clothes?" Steve asked as Corey closed the door.

"Naw, peep this, right. Big Lez just left. Wasn't nothing on Third Street, so she came by asking did I have any. So I gave her a twenty piece and got my dick sucked."

Suzie spoke up. "Excuse me, you have a female in the car."

"So, what? You're probably a pro your damn self."

Suzie's face turned purple. "Oh no, you didn't just say that, motherfuck—"

"Calm down, Suzie. You're wasting your time." Steve jumped in before things went overboard. "That's how he is, and it's why he can't keep a girl. He loves to tick people off."

Suzie slumped back in her seat, muttering, "Fucking with me, I'll…"

"You'll what? You better sit your ass in the front seat before I put you out," Corey challenged.

Steve shook his head, banging it on the steering wheel while Suzie huffed and puffed, her chest moving in and out as if she'd just run a marathon.

The only way to keep Corey quiet was for Steve to reach into the glove compartment and pull out a plastic bag filled with marijuana. When he passed it back, Corey lit up.

"I was just about to ask about that."

"Look in the side of your seat, you'll see a pack of Backwoods," Steve instructed. "Shut up and roll us one."

Corey turned to Suzie and, like a child asking for candy, said, "Suzie, dear, you don't mind if we smoke, do you, sweetheart?"

Suzie couldn't take it anymore. "Stop the car, Steve. Your friend is disrespecting me, and I don't appreciate it. Either he gets out, or I do."

"I hope you got some soft shoes on." Corey inhaled the smoke, then made a face, looking at the rolled-up marijuana. "'Cause your ass will be walking today."

Fed up, she grabbed the steering wheel and pulled. The car swerved across both sides of the road. Luckily, they were on a back street with no other cars coming or going.

Steve regained control, then pulled over on the side and stopped.

Suzie didn't waste any time getting out. Neither did Corey, who was in the front seat before the door slammed shut. It upset Steve, but he kept his calm. He drove the car alongside Suzie as she walked down the road.

"Why don't you get a brick and finish the job?" Steve hollered.

She stopped and turned to face them. "Look, Steve, I'm not going to sit in that car while your whatever-you-call-him of a friend keeps disrespecting me."

"Whatever, hoe," Corey butted in.

"Chill, Corey," Steve replied, but Corey's instant response came through, loud and sarcastic.

"No, man! These bitches thinks because they give you some pussy, you're supposed to glorify whatever they do. Let me tell you something, bitch! You think you love him, or he loves you, but love is me, his friend. I'm here for him, broke or rich, in or out of jail, violence or peace, sad or happy. Females come and go, but I'm always here. Once a niggah gets locked up or broke, you go right along about your business."

"He is right about that." Steve nodded.

"Well, if you think he's right, take him with you," she said.

And Steve drove off, looking back at Suzie in his rearview mirror. He felt bad, but not for her. Just for the loss of some good pussy.

Corey passed him the joint.

At the end of the block, Steve made a right turn onto Florida Avenue. Corey stretched across and turned on the heat, then lit another joint as Steve punched in one of his favorite CDs. They sang along, rocking their bodies and bobbing their heads, the car filled with smoke so thick it resembled a baby cloud. Before long, their eyes became bloodshot and red.

They rolled up to a stop light at the corner of Florida Avenue and Georgia Avenue. That particular intersection was always special for the boys, so they decided to sit and let the light change over again, causing confusion, but it was worth it. The two avenues were said to be the busiest on this side of town.

Georgia was known for the famous Howard University, which took up a large seven-block section of the street, starting at the corner on Florida. Then, there was Howard University Community Hospital, the Dentist Center, a mini plaza, a hotel, a McDonald's, Popeye's Chicken, the Howard College Apartments, a drug store, and the Benjamin Banneker Center.

Florida Avenue had its share of community affairs as the heart of the soul food movement. Seemingly endless shops of edible creativity, from pots and pans to the most Southern-style restaurants and hangout joints, ran all the way up to U Street. It also had a string of Afro-centric shops, including music and art. At the direct intersection of both avenues sat a Subway and a hair salon on one side, while the other side had a gift shop and another Popeye's Chicken.

With so much happening, anyone would want to sit and watch.

Then again, the real reason Steve and Corey chose to wait was the variety of girls to choose from. They loved the scenery, every shape and form. Even as they hung at the light, a cream-colored four-door Audi with two gorgeous black females pulled up alongside them.

They looked over at the guys, but just as Corey caught their look and was about to say something to Steve, he pulled off.

"Hey, man! Hold up! We've got two badass females behind us."

"Yeah, so are the damn cops!"

"Oh shit! Fuck them, then."

Steve didn't want the cops to get suspicious about them with the car as foggy as a steam room. The best thing to do was make it to the McDonald's before the pigs got a good glimpse. After all, it didn't look anything like car trouble or burning incense.

After making the right at the light on Georgia Avenue, Steve made a hard left into the parking lot. He parked the car in the first available space, then got out, glancing around for any sign of the cops, hardly able to see with those bloodshot eyes. Unable to get a good look, the next best thing was to go into or over by the McDonald's so they wouldn't be linked to the car.

As they proceeded across the parkway, the cream-colored car pulled up right in front of them. Corey initially thought they were the police and swallowed the joint sticking out of his mouth. Granted, they both stunk like a burned marijuana field.

The window on the passenger's side came down, and a female voice came out from the driver's side. The guys backed up just in case. Whether the girls had words they didn't want to hear or gunshots, they couldn't be too careful in D.C. Even ladies were doing drive-bys and jackings.

"Excuse me, cutie, what's your name?" It was the first time the girl-hoppers had heard someone else using their lines, especially a girl.

Corey ran around to the driver's side, eyeballing the flush-faced female driver—her short dark hair, beautiful big eyes, and of course, the voluptuous breasts coming out of her tight cat-like suit.

"Well, honey, I'll not only give you my name, but a juicy burger and a night by the fireplace with two blunts and a bottle of Don P."

"Do you seduce all your women like that?" The driver chuckled.

"Well, if you're gorgeous, and I like what I see, you deserve the best."

"I hope that's not all talk."

The other female in the car spoke up as she pointed at Steve. "What's wrong with your friend? Why is he so quiet?"

"I'm not quiet," said Steve. "Who's to tell, y'all might be feds."

"Trust me, cutie, I'll bend the rules and fuck you before I lock your ass up."

"Smooth talk won't get you anywhere. Action motivates me."

Corey saw how hot the conversation was getting, but he didn't want it to move too fast. After all, he hadn't even gotten to stage one with the driver. He knew how slick Steve could be, creaming the drawers right off a girl and leaving Corey standing by himself.

He moved to interrupt but was caught off guard when the driver opened her door and got out.

Her catsuit was so tight on her that he wondered how she was breathing. Granted, he was more concerned with the curves it showed off. His eyes moved down, holding a little bit longer on her feet. He loved a female with cute feet.

She caught him staring. "Is something wrong with my feet?"

"Oh, no! Honey, I love your feet, toes, and everything else."

She smiled at his remark, certain he meant what he said.

"Excuse me, honey, but my friend was rude for not telling y'all our names. I'm Steve, and he's Corey."

"Oh, please forgive us," said the driver. "We're the ones who were rude."

"That's okay. We would have gotten around to it eventually." Steve shrugged.

"My name is Paula," the driver said, then gestured to her passenger, "and that's my girl Kenya."

Steve got a little closer. From where he stood, he saw her cute smile, long hair, huge breasts, well-polished nails, and the same cat-like suit Paula wore. The only difference was its style. Hers ended in shorts, paired with some knee-high leather boots.

"Why don't you get out of the car and let me take a look at your outfit?"

"Why? So you can jump all over me? I'll let you see when we get to a more private place."

Steve's eyes grew wide, afflicted with both confusion and surprise. There sat some ready-to-go pussy taunting him.

What a time for a hard-on.

Instead of urging her to get out for him, he yelled at Corey and Paula as they leaned on the front of the car, getting acquainted with each other.

"Hey, youngin', these ladies need to be in a romantic setting, you feel me?"

"I've been feeling you since they pulled up."

"We can go to our apartment, if it's no trouble," said Kenya, smiling at Steve.

"Where do you beautiful creatures reside?" Corey asked.

"We go to Maryland University, so we live on campus in the co-ed apartments."

The guys looked at each other, then said in unison, "Maryland?!"

"Excuse me?" Paula huffed. "What's wrong with Maryland?"

"Hold up, don't get mad," Steven explained. "It's not the people that live in Maryland. It's the damn police. Them and Virginia hates every niggah in D.C., especially if you're young, black, and driving their yearly allowance."

"Plus," Corey added, "we got a gun and some weed, which we don't travel without."

"Well…" Kenya suggested, "just leave your car here and ride with us."

"Naw, better yet, I'll ride with Paula, and Kenya drives Steve's car. That is, if y'all ain't scared."

"If I was scared of anything, I wouldn't invite you to our house," said Kenya.

"That'll be straight! We can act like fake-ass married couples." Corey laughed.

After convincing themselves, they paired up and pulled off, one car behind the other.

Inside Paula's car, Corey couldn't keep his eyes off her. She saw him undressing her with his eyes, so she decided to help him a bit. She pulled down her zipper until it was dead center between her tits, making Corey's mouth water.

Imagining what he would do with those gorgeous globes in his mouth, he pulled a small bag from his sock, which contained marijuana and rolling papers.

"I hope you smoke," he said, grinning at her, "'cause I really need it right now."

"I bet you do."

"What do you mean by that?" When she didn't answer, he proceeded to roll himself a joint.

In the car behind them, Steve had his seat back, legs cocked up on the dashboard, and the sweet sounds of Anita Baker playing. One hand caressed Kenya, fingers tracing up and down the side of her neck to her forehead, the tip of her ear, and the side of her cheek. Aroused, she would let her fingers trail off the steering wheel and between Steve's legs whenever she could, and he loved it.

Up ahead, Paula and Corey made a right on New Hampshire Avenue. It was a busy street, mostly consisting of churches, parks, and middle-class houses. But it was quieter at night. Only the buses and cars that frequently ran through interrupted the calm on their direct link to the Maryland line.

If someone wanted to avoid traffic, a lot of stoplights, and most importantly in Steve and Corey's case, the fuzz, it was daily routine to keep up on the police's actions. Most of the time, in the boys' line of work, it was best to avoid cops as much as possible. Even though it was a safe route to Maryland, they still had to pass by their own stomping grounds. The corner where they sold drugs was considered a red-light zone where police frequently came through. One wrong move, and the district would be on them immediately.

After passing the hood, they couldn't wait to get across the line. By having guns in the car, they faced the problem of Maryland cops. Those guys played for keeps, which might be the ultimate challenge if they got pulled over.

Getting a gun charge and a drug charge together in Maryland was asking for a life sentence in prison without parole.

Inside Paula's car, Corey wasn't thinking about what might occur. All he wanted was some pussy. Plus, he was so high, all he did for the ride was smile and think about fucking Paula.

Steve was more alert, even while stoned. He didn't speak much on his way to the girls' house, partially paranoid, but also unwilling to interrupt the attention Kenya was giving his dick.

Kenya sensed something was wrong when he stopped playing with her ear and his body movements grew tense.

"Calm down, baby. We'll be there soon." She looked over at him. "Why don't you fire up a joint?"

He forced a smile, then proceeded to roll some weed.

In Paula's car, Corey didn't waste any time rolling up another joint.

"Do you want to hit this?" he asked Paula.

"If it's okay with you."

"What do you mean by that?"

"Your pretty ass smoked the last one all by yourself and didn't bother to ask me."

Corey cocked an eyebrow, confused. "I did too ask."

"No, you didn't. All you said was you hope I smoke."

"That's right, and it's your job to tell me to pass it."

"You're lucky I'm not a weedhead, or I'd put your ass out." Paula frowned.

Corey knew he was fucking up his chance, so he retreated.

"I'm sorry, sweetheart. Here, you fire this one up."

She took it and lit it as Corey kicked back in his seat, cracking a small smile. She was okay.

***

Between Eighth and Ninth Street, along Upshur, sat an alley. Nestled between the Chinese carryout and the variety store, the entrance faced the front of the Nigerian Store on Upshur and stretched back behind a bunch of houses, connecting to another entrance off one of the back streets.

Late in the evening, everyone hung out on the block. Buses, cars, and other vehicles moved along the intersection of Georgia Avenue and Upshur Street. People walked every which way, coming in and out of hair salons, barber shops, carryouts, variety stores, and all other manner of businesses.

That night, like all others, the alley was packed with a bunch of Steve and Corey's friends. Some sold drugs to passerby addicts. Others crowded in a circle, playing dice and throwing money in a pile. Those whose dice hit a certain number grabbed the cash, and the game started over. The ones on the other side hollered at females who were either getting off the buses, walking down the street, or coming out of one of the stores.

The main ones who hung out with Steve and Corey, their closest friends, were Kevin, Fat Al, Mike, Stokey, and Pee-Wee.

Kevin had a dark brown complexion, was five-foot-seven, and was naturally built at 170 pounds. He had a scar over his left eye, causing it to jump frequently. Always serious and keen, he'd been on edge ever since his last run-in with the cops.

Fat Al, on the other hand, was the total opposite of Kevin. At about five-four and a chubby 190 pounds, he kept his friends laughing, always cracking jokes on someone.

Mike was tall, dark, and even handsome in his own right. He seldom spoke to anyone outside of his friends and was the most cunning of the group.

Stokey was more on the conservative side. Involved in a steady relationship, he kept a balance in his lifestyle. Even though he made drug money, he believed he worked hard to get it. With a light brown complexion and wavy hair, his clean outfit sat well on his six-foot, 185-pound frame.

Pee-Wee was in the same league as Corey. They spent their days thinking about girls, but he liked to take it to the extreme. He didn't believe in catching diseases, nor did he care for the condom situation.

At a variety of ages between seventeen and twenty-one, they loved living the hood-kid's dream.

The day wasn't hot, but the weather seemed balmy since it was normally still cold at that time of the year. Nevertheless, it didn't stop the boys from going out and hustling.

Pee-Wee, Fat Al, and Kevin leaned on the car closest to the entrance of the alley. Standing there allowed them to observe everyone going in and coming out. If they didn't watch their backs, sometimes the undercover would show up unnoticed, sneak in, and eventually lock someone up.

Pee-Wee bent over and pulled up his jeans, reaching inside his socks and taking out a small Ziplock of marijuana. He then took off one of his boots and came out with an identical second bag.

He placed the two bags on the top of the car—Mike's metallic-blue Corvette—and reached into his leather jacket, repeating the routine.

"Damn, man!" Fat Al blurted out. "What you do, rob Bob Marley?"

Pee-Wee acknowledged his comment with a glance and smirk.

"I got the weed," the skirt-chaser said. "Somebody get the rolling papers or some blunts."

"I'm broke," Fat Al replied. "You brought the weed, so you can buy the blunts."

"Then your broke ass won't smoke," Pee-Wee snapped.

"Chill, y'all," Kevin interrupted. "With all the heads out here, someone's got the blunts."

Mike turned around from the gambling and commented, "Tell that fat freak to get the blunts. All he does is buy pussy."

"At least I fuck," Fat Al replied before heading toward the store. "We've never seen you with a female."

Mike just smiled and turned back to concentrate on gambling.

A car pulled up with six people in it. The driver waved at Kevin. In return, he jumped over the hood of the car he was leaning on and ran over to the entourage. After talking for a couple of minutes, he handed the lady some small pieces of a white substance. She gave him money, then drove off.

"Where's Corey and Steve?" he called as he came back. "I thought they would be out here by now. They know I can't hang out too long."

Mike yelled back from the gambling, "Just chill, youngin'. It ain't hot today. Haven't seen Blondie. Who were those broads, by the way?"

"It's this pipe-head me and Corey fucked one day."

"Damn, she looks too good to be smoking," replied Mike.

"I remember her telling Corey it's her husband's fault," said Kevin.

"She should get whooped for falling in, and he should get shot for fucking the sister up."

Walking out of the store, Fat Al heard Mike's comment to Kevin. "Come on, Mike, get real. One minute you're positive, then you're negative. You know damn well if that bitch comes up to you to buy a rock for a dick suck, you ain't thinking of no upliftment but to uplift your dick in her mouth."

Pee-Wee and the other guys burst into laughter.

The bag contained five or six boxes of cigars, which the group took out and dismembered. Even Fat Al joined in to compete to see who could roll the most and the best. After finishing up, they passed out the "greenie-green," everyone getting at least two or three blunts to themselves.

Suddenly, a crackhead came out of the alley, sweating, his clothes shabby and dirty. His face was black and greasy as if he'd been in an oil field. It was a familiar figure known to everyone as Shabby Joe.

He stumbled up to Pee-Wee.

"Look, man, I know I owe you. I got something to replace it." Joe's hands were shaking, his eyes wide open, as if he'd seen a ghost.

"It better be something worth my while, or I'm gonna beat you down," Pee-Wee warned.

"Don't worry! It's all you. All I ask for is a small piece."

"What is it?" Kevin asked.

"A case of Moet, Black Star."

Fat Al butted in with an enthusiastic, "Well, go get it, mo' fucker!"

Shabby Joe jetted around the corner, and in less than a minute, he came back with the case. Sweating even more, he placed the box down, rubbing his palms together.

Before Pee-Wee gave him a response about the case, Kevin jumped off the car and kicked Joe dead in the stomach. Then, in quick succession, Fat Al picked up a bottle and hit him upside his head.

When Joe started yelling for help, Pee-Wee stood over him, placing his hand over his face. Thinking Pee-Wee was about to do something even worse, the crackhead cowered. But instead, the dealer threw a piece of crack cocaine on him.

"I never told you when I was gonna beat your ass."

With a grin, he let him go, and Joe was gone. He didn't need to hear another warning.

The boys' laughter echoed after his retreating form.

CHAPTER FOUR

The evening was starting to tone down. A cool breeze picked up. Traffic was light, and most of the stores were closed, except the Chinese carryout and Mrs. Goine's Smorgasbord.

Business wasn't picking up for the boys, either. A few sales came by, but nothing to brag about: five-dollar bumps and ten-dollar dime pieces. Other than beating Joe's ass and gambling, there was nothing to pep up the evening. So they turned to everyone's all-time favorite, next to getting laid: leaning back on their cars, rolling, puffing, and passing.

Between puffs, Fat Al attempted to speak but couldn't. He was trying not to let the glorious marijuana smoke escape from his mouth or nostrils. He held up a finger, signaling the others to pay him some attention, eventually letting out what he could no longer hold.

"Man," he piped up, tears streaming from his eyes, "I saw Stokey's girl getting out of a Pathfinder when I was out doing my graveyard last night. Just like the one belonging to those First Street niggahs."

"I told Stokey that bitch wasn't any good," answered Pee-Wee.

"That fool isn't going to believe. He's in love," Kevin commented. He stood close to the alley. After too many close calls with Blondie, he wanted to be cautious.

"She wanted to give me the pussy before," added Mike.

"I'll be glad when you stop lying on your dick, Mike. All you fuck is pipe-heads," blurted Fat Al.

"It takes one to—"

Before Mike could finish his statement, loud music from Stokey's truck interrupted him. The tune was familiar; nothing the guys fancied, but after hearing nothing but good gospel songs coming from the vehicle, they got used it. The others looked at each other, then laughed.

"Hey, y'all!" Stokey jumped out of his truck and walked across the street, his happy mood shining through as he held up his hand and smiled at everyone. "Nice day, huh?"

Getting up from the dice game, Mike said, "Nice, my ass. It'll be cold in a minute."

Fat Al took a puff off his joint and studied Stokey before adding his two cents.

"Yo, Stokes, what's up with you and Kirk Franklin? I've never seen a drug-selling, weed-smoking, gospel-singing motherfucker."

"Don't knock him," remarked Mike. "He's no worse than those preachers who take Mom's money every Sunday, then play with boys all night."

"Don't mock me because I'm saved," Stokey retorted.

"Saved, my ass. You better check your history before grabbing onto some spook-ass religion," interrupted Pee-Wee.

Stokey got a bit upset with their mockery, but he kept smiling. "To hell with you. I believe in God. Too bad you don't."

"I don't really know too much about the Bible, or history," Kevin joined in, "but I read somewhere that the Bible we read today is contradictory. Plus, they say back in the day, Christianity was given to us as a sedative. Our forefathers were forced to obey the Bible that's still given to us."

"True indeed," said Pee-Wee. "After they were taken from Africa and robbed of their culture, religion, and freedom, they had no choice but to accept what the white man taught them."

"White man this, white man that... You damn right, it's the white man's fault!" blurted Fat Al. "Look around us! Our schooling's fucked up! They tell us Christopher Columbus discovered America, but they never teach us about the great blacks who helped create the world. They said in the Constitution that we're less than a man."

Stokey, unable to take it anymore, spoke up. "That doesn't mean we are what they say."

"I can't tell. Look at us! We sit here all day and sell drugs to our own kind. Genocide, brother." Fat Al chuckled. "Isn't it great how weed enhances the intellect of the mind?"

"Enough of this bullshit. Check this out." Stokey pulled a small box with a velvet covering out of his pocket. He opened it to show off a diamond ring.

"Oh, shit!" Fat Al crowed. "He not only got saved, but he's also dumb as fuck!"

"Don't knock me 'cause I'm ready to settle down. All you do is buy pussy, Fats."

Everyone broke into laughter, leaving Fat Al defeated and uncharacteristically silent for the first time all day. He knew Stokey was telling the truth.

"Don't jump too fast, Stokes," Kevin said amid the laughter. "Tell him what you saw last night, Al."

Fat Al didn't waste any time spilling the beans. After all, he was waiting for a chance to get back at Stokey. Plus, he loved to cause confusion.

"I saw your girl getting out of a niggah's truck, and it was a niggah we don't like, to boot."

"That's all? I know about that. He's her cousin."

"I told you he's in love," Kevin said with a smile.

Stokey held out the diamond for a couple of seconds longer, then replaced it back in his pocket. Pee-Wee, rather than say something to him, handed him the last rolled-up joint, which Stokey accepted with an even bigger smile.

Mike took a twenty-dollar bill out of his pocket and held it high in the air. Everyone knew what it meant. Before they could begin, however, tires screeched around the corner at full speed. The boys didn't have to think twice—they knew it was Blondie.

Stokey hastily ate the blunt, and Mike threw his gun on the roof. Fat Al, Pee-Wee, and everyone else stood still, but Kevin was already in the alley, heading for the other side. Blondie must have noticed because he heard the car heading straight for the alley.

Blondie pulled up halfway up the sidewalk and into the alley. She and Patterson jumped out, guns in hand. She didn't hesitate or look in the guys' direction, beelining straight after Kevin. Patterson opted to hold the others at gunpoint until she came back.

Toward the other end—not far from the exit to the street—Kevin neither ran nor walked. His aim was to move fast enough to keep his distance from both ends of the alley. He feared running into a police car at the other end but still checked to see if Blondie had popped around the corner. When she did, their eyes locked, and the chase began.

Kevin picked up speed, glancing back to gauge her pace. Noticing her gun wasn't out, he pulled his and fired.

Taken off guard, she jumped between a trash can and a pole, breathing heavily.

He was playing for keeps.

Stupid Jacob. Stupid Patterson. I can't focus with you two distracting me! I should've known this was coming, thought Blondie.

She immediately pulled her sidearm and rolled out on her stomach, both hands holding her weapon as she aimed down the barrel.

To her dismay, he was gone.

Blondie got up and brushed off. She was sweating uncontrollably, less from running than from Kevin's surprise. Again.

Next time, she thought, *I'll be more careful.*

Walking back, she tried to figure out where the bullets would've lodged. She knew it was an impossible task—the alley was filled with old cars, trash cans, and chopped pieces of wood—but she searched nonetheless. Gaining nothing, she eventually headed back to the car.

Back on the block, Patterson had the boys facing the wall with their hands on their heads. Seeing Blondie, he was relieved. He'd heard the shots, but Blondie hadn't called for backup, so he assumed everything was okay.

In his usual manner, Fat Al peeped from the corner of his eye to see how close Patterson was to him.

"Hey, ya!" Al taunted. "Check it out! Blondie got a new partner, and I think he's gay."

Mike added, "Did she tell you what happened to her last partner, Gimmy the Greek?"

"Shut up!" barked Patterson. "Did I tell you to speak?"

"If she told him," Pee-Wee muttered as Patterson looked up the alley at Blondie, "he wouldn't be her partner."

Blondie finally came close enough to speak, even though she was out of breath.

"The bastard got away. Let's go."

"What'll we do with these fuck-ups?" Patterson asked.

"Let them go. The one I wanted got away," answered Blondie.

***

Silent, she walked toward her vehicle and got in. Patterson followed without saying a word to the boys. Safe in the car, she asked if Patterson had found anything on them.

"Just some marijuana. That's all."

Blondie pulled off the curb, shaking her head.

"Don't bother with the misdemeanor paperwork. It keeps you away from the action on the street."

She got to the stop light on Georgia and Upshur, then made a left, passing a gas station next to a striptease bar with a Jewish owner.

As her car went by, she shook her head at the sight of the half-naked girls parading around the front entrance. She knew most of them weren't old enough, but it wasn't her problem, anyhow.

She proceeded down the avenue as the sun went down and the chilly night air set in. On her left, in between Taylor and Shepard Street, sat the Red Top store—the hangout spot for the Jamaicans.

She suspected some happenings but couldn't pinpoint it. The loyalty code and secrecy among them was too strong, and it burned her not to know more. Every day, all sorts of vehicles, numbers ranging from a couple hundred to nearly a thousand, would gather up at the store and sometimes didn't leave until six in the morning. She remembered her superior talking about the shop, but they couldn't get an inside connection to find out what was going on.

Even as they continued toward the Plaza by Howard University, Blondie sensed Patterson beaming her down with his eyes.

She glanced at him and said, "If you want to lock them up that bad, we can turn around."

Patterson placed one arm on the windowsill, his chin resting in his hand, like *The Thinker*. He looked at Blondie with concern, the boys' jokes echoing in his mind.

Blondie repeated herself, jolting him out of the thought.

"No, I'm over that. It's what the boys said that's bothering me."

"And what would that be?"

"Oh, nothing serious. They only mentioned someone named Gimmy the Greek?"

At the sound of the name, Blondie hit the brakes and pulled into the nearest gas station on the avenue. She slammed her hands on the steering wheel, tears erupting down her cheeks.

"Alright," she cried out. "Alright!"

Patterson sat there in amazement, staring at her. She looked as if someone had killed a part of her. Her breathing rapid and her hands shaking, she clenched the steering wheel with force.

Patterson touched her shoulder gently. She took a moment to get ahold of herself.

"That kid, Kevin. He killed Gimmy. But it was my fault. I choked. It was my first time on the road, and Gimmy thought I was ready." She got quiet for a moment as the horrifying memories returned in vivid detail to her mind. She heard the gunshots echoing as if she were there again.

Patterson understood her anger, so before speaking, he chose his words carefully. "So that's why you're after the kid."

"Well, the little fucker's been doing a lot more since then."

"If you want him so badly, we can just bring him in."

She took both hands and ran them through her hair, looking into the mirror. She hated talking about the situation, but she kept the conversation going just to satisfy Patterson.

"We did bring him in, but with no gun and no one willing to testify, the case was closed."

"Wait a minute, you're telling me he did this in front of witnesses?"

"It was my first day in the field. Gimmy took me to what he called Dodge City Lane, right where we just left. Don't be fooled by the appearance. That neighborhood can get real raunchy.

"Anyway, we pulled up one evening on a regular roundup. We came through an alley and saw some guys selling what seemed to be crack cocaine to these civilians in a blue pickup. When they saw us, they didn't run. They just… stood there, looking at us. When Gimmy jumped out of the car and told them to freeze, all they did was smile. Something seemed off.

"As Gimmy walked up to them, the truck drove away. That's when I heard shots. I didn't see Gimmy fire. He turned to face me, and all I saw was blood dripping from his head. I froze in the car. I couldn't move. But I noticed three boys running down the alley. The one with the gun looked back at me. He smiled, pointed the gun at me, then ran."

"The one with the gun was Kevin?" Patterson asked.

"Yeah… and that son of a bitch is gonna pay."

***

Back on the block, the boys relaxed and got back to business. They knew Blondie's schedule; she wouldn't be back until late, and by then, everyone would be doing their own thing.

Mike climbed up on the roof of the tire shop and retrieved the gun he'd thrown. Everyone down below got their jackets out as the sun disappeared and the cool evening air picked up.

"Let's find some freaks and get a hotel room," Fat Al suggested.

"I second that. It'll be fucked if I get locked up on a night like this," Pee-Wee agreed.

Another one of their friends, Bennie, came out of the store with two six-packs of Heineken and rolling papers. He didn't comment on what was said; he knew what was up.

With everyone getting ready to drive off, none of them noticed the blue Nova steadily creeping down the street with all four of its windows down.

Before it got too close, Mike's head snapped around. His experienced eye picked up on the telltale signs.

"Drive-by!"

Bullets riddled the street, hitting cars, a few lodging in the front door of the store. Fat Al retaliated, running out of the alley with an Uzi and firing at the Nova, which sped off, broke the stoplight, and kept going.

"Is everybody alright?" Mike called out.

To his relief, most of the guys were just shaken, but it wasn't anything to get hysterical about. Just normal, day-to-day routine.

Pee-Wee answered, "Yeah, but let's roll before Blondie comes back. We'll deal with them niggahs later."

"Chill. You don't have to move too fast. The people around here aren't going to tell," Stokey piped up.

"You can tell that to your lawyer," Pee-Wee spat back.

Without any more argument, they got in their cars and left.

CHAPTER FIVE

The sun dropped completely out of sight, the chill of the evening settling in. The wind picked up as the temperature fell, and both cars entered a large complex with a strict security entrance and computerized cameras. Corey and Steve felt safer, but they never knew what could happen in Maryland.

They parked in designated spaces, got out, and entered the building.

Rule one, Steve thought as he walked to their apartment, *is it might be a set-up.*

He felt under his jacket to make sure his gun was in the right place. Corey, on the other hand, was too busy kissing all over Paula, his dick in control of his actions as they climbed two flights of stairs to the girls' apartment.

Inside, it was beautifully decorated; the living room was all green wallpaper with a matching love sofa. The blinds, green with gold trimmings, meshed with the coffee table sitting in the center of the room, which was made of glass and graced with a green cat statue with gold eyes and paws. On each of the four corners sat miniature gold kittens to complete the look. To the far left stood an entertainment set: TV, radio, 24-CD player, and a VCR with surround sound, all covered in green and gold. To the far right, the minibar shone, lined with champagne bottles of every kind. In the middle of the bar stood a punch bowl surrounded by mini flutes with crystal and gold trimmings.

Opposite the bar was the two-way kitchen, decked out in checkered black-and-white floors, a table, and high stools sitting at an L-shaped counter.

Seeing the girls' layout, the boys smiled at each other. Jackpot.

Corey's genitals took a break, his favorite body part making a call instead. After smoking so much on his way there, his stomach responded. "What's in the refrigerator?"

Paula pointed to the kitchen and said, "Help yourself. I'm going to change."

"Me too," echoed Kenya, and they both disappeared down the small hallway to the bedrooms.

Corey didn't waste any time exploring the kitchen and its accessories. He found plenty.

"Hey, slim," he called back to Steve, "these females ain't half-ass bad."

Steve was too busy with the remote to respond, clicking from one station to another and settling on the History Channel.

A few minutes later, the girls sauntered into the living room. Kenya wore a transparent silvery mini negligee with matching panties. Her nipples peeked through teasingly as her supple breasts hung free without a bra to suppress them.

Paula followed her in, her outfit much like Kenya's, swirling as she walked, and showing off even more as her bare abdomen and thighs winked between the sheer folds of fabric.

Steve, astonished as well as surprised, smiled and kept his cool.

Meanwhile, Corey missed their entrance, busy cooking up something to eat, the weed turning him into a chef.

Kenya took a seat beside Steve, and his hard-on came back immediately, while in the kitchen, Paula walked up behind Corey and slid her hand under his shirt. He tensed for what seemed to be forever, then slowly turned around. Seeing how she was dressed, he almost burned his hand. She winked at him, then turned to leave, but he held her hand and pulled her toward him.

In the living room, Kenya positioned herself on the couch and asked Steve to sit between her legs. As she crossed both legs around his waist and wrapped her arms around his chest, she saw Steve's choice of programming and raised an eyebrow.

"You're the first boy I've met that watches the History Channel. What's up with that?"

"My mom got me liking this shit. She said it was good brain power… you can learn a lot."

"Huh… What's this about?"

"Some guy named Joseph Stalin. He's supposed to be one of the wickedest guys that lived. He had a bunch of famers and commies killed."

"Kinda like Hitler, right?"

"Yeah. They said he probably killed even more people than Hitler."

Reaching for the remote, she said, "Enough about that. Find B.E.T."

She clicked through the stations, then paused at the Sex Channel. Some couple was getting their groove going on a couch just like the one they occupied. They looked at each other with a twinkle in their eyes.

Kenya began to say something but was interrupted by Steve's finger on her lips. As she licked his finger slowly, he turned around and kissed her nipple through the outer layer of her negligee. He worked his way down to her navel. As he got to the panties, his head was lost between the warmth of her thighs. He positioned himself on his knees, holding both legs in the air as he gently sucked through her silk underwear, eliciting uncontrollable twitching from her hips.

Hitting his pace, he pulled the panties off, licking her love button.

She shivered at the touch of his tongue, her juices flowing instantly. She grabbed his head and let out a low moan of excitement.

Corey was busy eating his own menu, but instead of steak and eggs, it was hot meat seasoned by a special sauce flowing from Paula's inner thighs. He propped her up on the table, spread-eagle.

The apartment was filled with love and the smell of down-home cooking. Both fragrances cultivated happiness. Without interrupting Kenya and Steve, Corey and Paula slipped by.

In Paula's bedroom, Corey undressed in seconds, his beeper falling on the floor. He picked it up and threw it on the night table before he jumped all over Paula, kissing at her body with passion and eagerness.

His beeper went off, but he didn't pay it any mind. However, the constant buzzing of the device on the table interrupted his concentration. He reached for it to cut it off, then noticed the number. It was his homie's code; that code had to be answered whether it was business or pleasure.

His excitement faded. He rolled over and sat on the side of the bed. Picking up the phone, he dialed. It rang a few times before Mike answered.

***

It was six p.m. when Christopher's mother walked into his room. She sat on his bed, waiting for him to exit the bathroom. As he came out, he noticed her concerned look.

"What's up, Mom?"

"Sit down for a minute, son." She patted the bed beside her. "You know I love you very much, and I wouldn't want for you to get back in trouble."

"I know, Mom." Christopher leaned over and hugged his mother. "I knew this was coming, but you have nothing to worry about."

"It's not you. It's the changes that place can bring to a young man like yourself."

"I know not to get in trouble. This time, I'll think first."

"Talk is cheap. I want to be able to trust you."

Getting up from beside his mother, Christopher knelt in front of her, taking both of her hands in his.

Looking up into her eyes, he said, "You can trust me, Mom."

"Hurry up, Chris!" Carol yelled through the door, breaking the moment.

His mother smiled, kissing him before she got up to leave.

Looking into his mirror, he thought about her expectations of him this time around. With his sister yelling for him to come on, he took one last look, then ran out of the room.

In the living room, he met Reggie, who wasn't what Chris had expected. He was striking, both in his attitude and appearance, with the tall, dark, and handsome figure he knew his sister liked.

Next to him sat the lustrous Cherry. She looked like something out of one of the magazines he'd had in the joint, leaving Chris speechless.

Carol didn't give anyone the chance to get formal. She had the door open, gesturing for everyone to hurry out.

Cherry eyed Chris from head to toe as he walked out of the house, a small smirk on her face.

Riding in the car, Chris felt a bit uneasy. He found it hard to get acquainted with Reggie and Cherry. His only conversation would be about prison, and he had doubts about bringing it up so early.

Fortunately, Cherry decided to break the ice.

"So, what's up, Chris? You haven't said a word since we got in the car."

"Don't blame me if I don't know what to say."

"Say anything. Tell me about the joint. Is it as bad as they say?"

"Only if you want it to be."

"Hey, Chris," Reggie added, "how about working at the restaurant with me?"

"No, thanks. I don't want to be a waiter."

"Not a waiter. Just to help me in the office and run errands for me."

Carol looked over at Chris. "That way, you'll have a job to calm Mom down. She'd be proud."

Cherry put her arm around his neck, whispering, "You got a job… How about being my boyfriend, too?"

Chris tensed up and turned his face toward the window. Yet another big problem that he had to deal with sooner or later.

They arrived at a nightclub with an attached restaurant called Tiffany's. They decided to eat first, then get their party on. Cherry held Chris's hand to assure him that everything was okay as she guided him inside.

After dinner, Carol suggested they see a movie since it was still early, so they went to see an action flick before coming back to party the night away.

At nearly three a.m., it was finally getting late.

"We should be going," Reggie mentioned to Carol as they rested at the table. "I have a business meeting in the morning."

Cherry agreed, as she too had plans, though it wasn't a business meeting. She launched those dreamy eyes at Christopher. He felt her beams and got even more uneasy.

His problem was coming sooner than he'd expected.

On their way home, Reggie stopped off at Cherry's house first. She stepped out of the car, then turned back.

"Why is you still sitting in the car?" she asked Chris. "Aren't you gonna come in?"

Feeling shy and surprised, his only answer was, "No, I'm okay. I'll just go straight home."

Carol reached over and pushed him toward the door with a smile on her face. "Go ahead, stupid. Me and Reggie will come back and get you."

Chris was cornered. He couldn't back out, so he slowly edged his way out of the car. By the time his feet hit the pavement, Cherry was standing with her front door open. He glanced back at his sister. She knew the thoughts running through his mind and waved, an encouraging smile on her face. Climbing up the steps into the house, Chris took one last full breath before he walked past Cherry. She closed the door and gestured for him to sit on the couch.

As she clicked on a few lights, he noticed how cozy her house was set up. A plush sofa, matching love seat, and neat wallpaper. Beautiful paintings decorated the walls, and the carpet was white and thick underfoot.

She walked in front of him and bent over to pick up the remote. Her curvaceous ass was giving him a hard-on. She turned to give him the remote, a smile on her face, and walked off toward her bedroom. Palms sweating, Chris wondered if Cherry knew he was a virgin. Then he wondered if *she* was a virgin. With how fast things were moving, he doubted it. His nerves intensified. How could he compete with the guys she'd been with before?

Chris's first instinct was to jet for the door, but he battled against it. There had to be a first time, or his problem would go unsolved. He was ready.

Cherry came out of the bedroom wearing her nightgown cut way above her knees. She purposely sat in front of Chris, legs apart, so he had a clear view of her skimpy G-string that barely covered her pussy. The sight of hair coming from the sides of her thigh made Chris start to sweat.

Cherry noticed his uneasiness. "Why haven't you taken off your coat?"

"I'm okay. Carol will be back soon."

Leaning forward, she reached toward Chris, sliding both arms around his neck. Engulfed by her sweet aroma and the softness of her juicy mounds, he couldn't get away if he wanted to.

"Either you give me the virgin dick," she whispered seductively, "or I'm gonna take it."

"So…" He swallowed. "So you knew all along, huh?"

"I knew before you came home, and I'm determined to be your first. Let's go in the bedroom." Cherry stood up and grabbed him by the jacket. "Class is in session."

She led him to the bedroom. Inside, she wasted no time undressing him right down to his underwear. She smiled at the size and thickness of his hard-on as it poked her in the face.

Without hesitation, she took him in her mouth. After moving up and down on his manhood a few times, he couldn't help but lose all of his anxiety. She stood up and licked her lips, clearing her mouth.

"This is gonna be the best and longest night of my life." Cherry dropped her nightgown and sat on the bed, her hand outstretched, beckoning Chris. As he lay down beside her, she turned to him and smirked. "The first lesson of the day is foreplay…"

Chris gave himself to Cherry in total submission. She did and taught him things only his imagination could conceive. The rest of the night was filled with soaked sheets, tangled bodies, and the throes of riveting climax.

After lying there for what seemed like eternity, Cherry's legs wrapped around him, her head on his chest, the phone rang. She reached across him and picked it up.

"Hello?"

"Yo! Cherry, what's up? Everything alright?" Carol asked.

Smiling, Cherry answered, "I'll let you ask him that," then passed Chris the phone.

"What's up?" Chris said.

"Are you ready for me to come get you?"

"Hell, no! I'll see you at the house. Cherry ain't finished schooling me."

"Is that right? Let me speak back to her."

Chris passed the phone back, and Cherry laughed. "Don't blame if it's the best."

"I don't care about the best. Just don't have my brother strung out over there."

Reggie interrupted in the background, "Tell Cherry to drop him by the restaurant tomorrow."

"Reggie says to bring him by the restaurant—"

"I heard him. Look, you're taking up time. Our lunch break is over. See you in the morning." She hung up the phone without giving Carol a chance to reply.

She then rolled over, looking Chris in the eye as she mounted his already-erect member. Leaning forward, she kissed all over his chest, biting his nipples while riding his manhood to a frenzy.

Chris's erotic adventure had him in shock, even after hours of schooling. Every second with Cherry was fabulous. From then on, she was his world.

It was eight fifteen when Cherry's alarm clock went buzzing. As she rolled out of bed and walked to the bathroom, Chris was already awake and staring at the ceiling.

"Couldn't sleep, huh?"

"Yeah, I slept, but in the joint, you get used to waking up early. You work today or something?"

"I'm a hairdresser. I don't have to be in until nine a.m. That's my first scheduled appointment."

"Big Wilma style, huh?"

"Boy, shut up and come on over here."

"Is the bathroom another part of class?"

"It can be if you hurry up."

In seconds, he was in the shower with her, making more bubbles. She had to cut it short, or they may have never gotten out of the house.

While dressing, Cherry said, "I'm sorry that I can't make you one of my favorite omelets."

"That's fine. Whatever you served, I'm still full."

They left the house and drove off in her car. Twenty minutes later, they pulled up in front of a large building off a busy street. The front of the building had big tinted glass that ran from one corner of the building to the next.

The name was the first thing Chris noticed as they pulled up: *The Rontourante-La-Rogue.* A French name. He glanced at Cherry, and she automatically knew what was on his mind.

"That's Reggie's trick for pulling people in. He says after coming in and smelling down-home cooking, you won't want to leave."

Cherry reached over and kissed him. She felt his manhood rising and put her hand between his legs, grabbing what she owned. He hurriedly opened the door and got out before he changed his mind about getting a job.

Stepping out and walking to the front door, he stared into the window before going in. Once more, he looked up at the name of the restaurant and smiled to himself.

He pushed through double glass doors with gold writing printed upon them. The front entrance was lined with black-and-gold curtains. His eyes had to adjust to the scenery due to the sunlight outside. He walked along a few tables before seeing Reggie with some guys sitting at a corner booth.

He wondered if he'd come too early. Reggie was in a meeting and probably wouldn't have time for him. Next to them was another set of double doors that led to the kitchen. Since he hadn't had breakfast and didn't want to cause a fuss, he reckoned Reggie wouldn't mind him getting a bite to eat. As he walked up the corridor, he noticed Reggie neither spoke nor waved to him.

His first instinct was to go over, but then thought against it, deciding to head for the kitchen first. But to his dismay, he encountered something completely unexpected. A huge, husky figure got up from the table with Reggie and headed his direction. As the figure got closer, the guy pulled a shiny object from the inside of his jacket and pointed it at Chris.

All Chris heard behind the man was Reggie's voice saying, "Come on, man, not the kid. He's innocent."

"Yeah?" a Spanish-looking guy in a bright yellow suit chuckled. "So why is he here so early?"

"I told him to come. I offered him a job."

"I bet that job was to bump us off, huh!"

CHAPTER SIX

Mike's voice echoed through the phone. "Hey, man, meet us at the playground. Can't talk long. Bye."

Putting down his cell, Corey called out to Steve, "Yo, Steve, I think them niggahs in trouble."

Out in the living room, Steve and Kenya were busy munching on each other's genitals, locked in the sixty-nine position. He had to come up for air to answer.

"Gimme a minute. I'm almost finished."

"It's some serious shit," Corey replied, walking into the living room in spite of the two naked bodies on the carpet. "Mike sounded fucked up."

Steve sighed and got up, pulling his boxers on as Kenya watched, her eyes widening with disbelief.

"Don't be mad. My dogs come first."

"I won't be, if you promise to come back."

Smiling at her, he said, "Yeah, I'll definitely do that."

Corey walked out of the bedroom dressed and ready to go, closely followed by Paula. He and Steve each kissed the girl they came with, then left.

They got back to D.C in record time. Fifteen minutes later, they double-parked in front of The Foxy Playground.

To them, The Foxy Playground was their meeting office. But to the public, it was the spot for naked girls, topless lap dances, and side shows with play toys. Dark on the inside and not too far from the drug spot, the boys made it their personal clubhouse for both business and pleasure.

As Steve and Corey entered, they were greeted by a few of the dancers who knew them well. They hugged, squeezing a few butts to show the girls their appreciation. Then, they went straight to the others, who were waiting for them under the forty-four-inch theater vision at the far back-right of the club.

They walked up, slapping everybody fives. "Hey, fellas. What's up?"

Fat Al, the hero of the day, spoke up first.

"Man, you should have been there. Them niggahs almost had us."

"Oh shit, shoot-out, huh? Anybody get hit?" asked Steve.

"Naw," Mike answered, "but Kevin disappeared when Blondie chased him through the alley."

"Hold up... don't tell me y'all was doing it with Blondie?"

"Naw man, it was after Blondie pulled up," answered Fat Al. "I think them bammas was watching us the whole time."

"Did she catch Kevin?"

"I don't think so. We would've heard by now."

"So, what's up? Get back, or what?" Corey asked.

"That's why we beeped ya," answered Mike.

Corey turned to Pee-Wee, who was making eye contact with one of the dancers. Tapping him on the shoulder, he asked about what had happened to the girls from before.

"Man, they kept beeping me all day! Then this shit came down, and now they got to wait," Pee-Wee complained.

"I say we get those thugs now, while it's early," Stokey interrupted, coming back from the bathroom. "Them suckers won't know what hit them."

Fat Al cocked his head. "Broad daylight, huh?"

"Yeah, slim, broad daylight!" chimed Mike.

"Let's get the joints and do this," Steve agreed, getting up from his seat.

Fat Al sat there for a second and thought about it, but he couldn't object. He couldn't tell the guys how he felt about going out in broad daylight. After all, the comedy he used to talk about was becoming a reality.

They all left the club one by one to avoid the suspicion of the girls or customers. Not only was the club their private space, but it was also a haven to their number-one enemy, the police. A lot of undercover and off-duty officers frequented the club. It was a chance the boys played with because it had its values, and they were always prepared. With the help of the dancers that they knew well who would point out all the police, they avoided capture. This was also good if they encountered an officer on the street because there was a chance they already knew the motherfucker.

Across the street, directly in front of the club, was an alley. At the end sat an abandoned house. Everyone met inside, down in the basement, where they kept their guns and ammunition. Taking a seat, they chose their favorite weapons then headed out through the back door to the "buckets"—old cars that no longer belonged to anyone. They separated in three cars, splitting up in case they had a run-in with the police. Driving down Kansas Avenue, approaching Sixteenth Street, they took to the alleys and side roads.

Two blocks from where their enemies hung out, to everyone's surprise, they saw Stokey was right on cue. The busters were standing around without a care in the world, the neighborhood jumping with people. It would be great for a major drive-by.

Without hesitation, they crept down the block, unnoticed until it was too late. The other guys didn't realize what hit them. The three cars unloaded their shots, then took off down the street, making the first left turn that took them back to the avenue. But instead of returning to their neighborhood, they went in the opposite direction, toward their favorite McDonalds.

Steve's car was the first in the drive-through, slowing down as he pulled up to the intercom. Winding down the window, he yelled back to everybody, "Don't even think about going back to the hood because we ain't."

Pee-Wee heard Steve's remark and called back, "I don't care where we go. Let's just get rid of those joints before we get pulled over."

"I got somewhere. Just get your shit and let's go," said Steve.

He was about to pull off to wait for the others when the beautiful smile one of the female attendants stopped him in his tracks.

"Hey, check out that dime piece." He attempted to get out of his car but realized he had to move out of the way so the other cars wouldn't be blocked.

He quickly parked, got out of his car, and ran back to the window.

"Excuse me. This is gonna sound kinda strange… Can I borrow a quarter?"

She looked at him with a frown and asked, "For what?"

"So I can call my mother to let her know I just fell in love."

Smiling at him, she looked him straight in the eye and said, "I think you should take that lame-ass line back where you got it."

"Damn! At least I tried. Plus, I made you smile."

"Tried? You call that tried?"

"Hold up, baby girl. Two things I don't chase after are women and buses, so don't stand here and act like you're the shit. I can do better elsewhere."

"Well fine. I'm not pressed," she said, waving her hand in his face.

Steve had never come across a female who made him persist. He tried again with a different approach, smiling. "See what love can do to a couple?"

"Love? Boy, please, you don't know me from a can of paint. What you do? Go around falling in love with strangers?"

"Gimme time. Something might happen."

The conversation was interrupted by his buddies blowing their horn, letting him know they were ready. He grabbed a piece of paper, wrote his beeper number down, then handed it to her.

"Here's my number. Hit me up later. We need to finish this."

Before she could respond, he ran off. She stared after him with the piece of paper in hand.

"Finish what?" she murmured in a low tone.

Riding down New York Avenue, each car followed one behind the other as they approached the 495 Beltway leading to the Baltimore-Washington parkway. Steve's car took the lead. They rode past two exits, then turned off on the third for Landover.

Fat Al thought to himself how crazy the whole thing was. He was better taking his chances in D.C. than in Maryland. But rather than make a comment, he kept to himself and enjoyed the ride.

After a few minutes of driving through Maryland, Steve turned into the parking lot of the same high-rise condominiums. They were both built the same; the only difference was in color, each adding glamour and elegance.

Steve stopped in front of the second to last of the row's condos, got out, and walked straight to the front door.

The others didn't follow.

In the doorway, he was greeted by a beautiful female in a white silk robe. She kissed him, then gave him a hug, the others looking on in curiosity. Then, he motioned with his hand for them to follow him. They all piled out of their rides and headed for the house, walking straight in without even introducing themselves.

Steve led them all downstairs. He turned on the stereo and took out champagne, and everybody followed suit by pulling out blunts packed with weed and smoking at their leisure. A couple of guys busied themselves with a video game.

With all the commotion, Kia came downstairs wearing a tight dress that clung to her thighs. She motioned for them to cut the music down.

Steve looked at her and licked his lips.

The others stared at her as well, wide-eyed. She looked juicy.

Steve got up and walked over to her.

"You like this, babe?" she whispered in his ear.

He licked his lips again, and she understood full well.

When he asked, "Can I take it off you?" she turned and slowly walked back up the steps. He followed.

"This must be the broad he's in love with," Stokey said with a smile.

"Might be. I've never heard him talk about this one," replied Corey.

"She's alright, but I like the house better," Fat Al commented.

"When they come back down, I'mma ask her for a friend," blurted Pee-Wee.

"Don't no woman want you," said Mike as he passed the joint.

"We'll see about that! Don't player-hate, 'cause I'm the shit when it comes to women."

After a while, Kia and Steve reappeared, Steve only wearing his shorts.

Pee-Wee jumped up and asked her, "What's up with a friend for me, Kia?"

"Sorry, my friends aren't interested in hoodlums."

"You got Steve."

"Everybody has different tastes."

"So you shouldn't speak for them. Let them check the merchandise."

"Ya act too young."

"I act according to the female."

"Don't get mad, and remember I warned you."

"Let me worry about that."

Fat Al asked Kia, "Why you not at work today?"

"None of your damn business," she snapped.

"Damn! Just trying to make conversation."

"Don't do it with me. Go read a book."

"What the fuck is wrong with her? She be flipping," said Fat Al.

"Chill out, Al." Steve sighed. "She's fucked up with me."

"I thought for a minute she was all clogged up."

Everybody but Kia laughed. Instead, she turned and went back upstairs.

"She's mad because she thinks I'm running around on her," Steve said, sitting down.

Corey almost spit out his drink. "Man, doesn't she know we're players?"

"Plus, she's giving you the pussy," stated Mike. "You know how females get about that type of shit."

"Man, we from the hood! We don't cater to that lovey-dovey commitment shit," said Fat Al.

"That's what happens when you come across a mature woman," Stokey interjected.

They sat around for the end part of the evening, chatting, smoking, and playing video games. But eventually, the conversation led to more serious topics.

"Since we're all here feeling good, I want you to keep in mind what might happen if someone sees us, or we get caught one day." Steve was the one who always engaged in that type of talk, just to keep the others up on their negativity. He never told them how to think, but he always pointed out possibilities.

"Oh shit, here we go! Judge and jury!" shouted Fat Al.

"Naw, I'm for real! These days, the courthouse isn't set up to give us a break. The feds have all jurisdiction under control. And when you're black, you guilty until proven innocent."

"Not today, Steve," Fat Al interrupted. "Y'all notice whenever we're together, he always wants to preach?"

"If I don't let you know, who will?"

"We have the school, maybe the preacher," stated Al. "If you stayed in long enough, you'd know."

"It's not school. I say society."

"Why society? You made the decision," said Mike.

"I'm glad you said that! Because the day you get fucked, we each have a decision to make."

"And what's that?" asked Pee-Wee.

"Cooperate, or go hard."

"Cooperate? Man, who the hell you think we are? Ain't no feds on this planet'll can me." Fat Al laughed. "Shit, I don't do too much reading or know the law, but these days, the only way the feds break a motherfucker down is through someone in the circle."

"We ain't those people. Fuck the feds, I'm going out hard," said Corey.

"A lot of people look at us like savages with no train of thought," replied Steve as he passed the blunt.

"They want us to be like they used to," stated Corey.

"Hell, look at the shit we do," answered Mike.

"The white man couldn't be perfect or like Jesus. Look what he taught me to do! Kill my brothers, sell drugs, and disrespect my sisters," stated Fat Al.

"I say the government is God, not Jesus," said Corey.

"What makes you think Jesus is God?"

"I said God, not Jesus. I know the difference."

"Talk about women," Fat Al huffed. "Fuck the white man."

"You can't," Mike announced. "He's fucking us."

"Hey, they say the woman is our earth. The womb is like the universe, and our great affection is her. Why not praise her?" Pee-Wee smiled.

"Speaking of woman," stated Fat Al, "I know your girl has some good pussy, huh, Steve?"

Before Steve got a chance to answer, Mike butted in. "You see," he said, pointing at Al. "Why I be cussing this fat mothafucker out? His freak ass sitting here thinking about your girl."

"Steve knows I don't mean nothing by it, huh, bro? So is it good or what?"

"You make it sound like we a bunch of bitches sitting around discussing dudes," replied Mike.

"They do it, so why can't we?"

"All pussy is good pussy, take it from me. It's just the person connected to the pussy," Pee-Wee asserted.

"You got life fucked up," said Mike. "Some pussy is pure garbage."

"How you know? We ain't never seen you with a girl, not counting crackheads," laughed Fat Al.

Mike jumped up, chasing Fat Al around the room. He caught him, wrestling him to the floor. Everyone laughed.

In the midst of the chaos, Stokey called Steve over.

"I was thinking, right? What you said about religion and shit… So you're telling me, if Jesus wasn't white, that mean the Bible is kinda fucked up, huh?"

"Well, I tell you like this, first go research for yourself. Don't believe me, 'cause one, they say the Bible been around since the beginning of time, but it only goes back as far as two thousand years. It was never mentioned during the days of the pyramids, so as far as I'm concerned, it's just a good book to read if you study it well."

"Wait a minute… If the Bible is off track, what about Christianity?" Corey butted in eagerly.

"Oh man! Y'all are getting too deep. What's up with the Koran?" asked Fat Al.

"Personally, I think it's a good one to read, too. Don't get me wrong. They're some good books, but not something to base your whole life around."

"So what do you suggest we read, study, and learn from?" Mike prodded.

"Do they have other books that enlighten you the same way?" asked Stokey.

"Sure! There's books like *The Browder Files, Superman to Man, They Came Before Columbus* by Dr. Ivan Van Sertima and our homegirl Dr. Frances Cress Welsing. They have some pretty interesting stuff to read."

"So you saying if we read more and find ourselves, dudes like us wouldn't be doing the shit we do now?" stated Mike.

Pee-wee got up to use the phone, leaving the others to their philosophizing.

"You know all this shit and you ain't changed," argued Fat Al.

"One person can't change the world," answered Steve.

Pee-Wee came back and smiled at Corey, who perked up. "That's them, huh?"

"Yup. Whenever you're ready."

As Corey and Pee-Wee removed themselves from the conversation, Kia came downstairs with a duffel bag.

"Where do you want me to put the guns?" she asked.

"Put them up. We're chilling for the night."

"She's gonna keep the guns? Suppose we run into them niggahs tonight!" Fat Al looked at everyone in astonishment.

"Let me answer that, Steve," said Pee-Wee. "Well, fatso, me and Corey has a date, Stokey is going over to his girl's house, Steve's staying here, and Mike, well, that's another story."

"Man, I can't go home! I've got drugs to sell. You know I'm trying to buy a car," Al complained.

Steve walked over to Fat Al, grabbed him by both shoulders, and looked him straight in the eye.

"How about we give you all the guns to take back, you have no license, and when you get locked up, just don't call any of us to come get you."

"Okay. If you put it that way, I think we should leave them here."

His statement drew out a chuckle from the others.

***

Driving back up the avenue in total silence, neither officer looked at or said anything to the other. Both were lost in thought as they entered the back parking lot of the station. No one exited at first. They sat for a minute, gathering up their belongings. Patterson knew his new partner would be an interesting subject to work with, maybe more interesting than the streets themselves.

They finally got out, walking to the back entrance as Patterson broke the ice.

"Today was interesting. I learned a lot about your neighborhood."

"Well, that's nice to hear, but you haven't seen the worst. There's still Big Dre, the top dealer. Then, at times, the street beefs stir up, and that's when it gets hectic."

"You mean like what happened today on Fourteenth Street?"

"Sometimes. Sometimes worse."

"How much worse can it get? Three people got killed, and two injured."

"What's worse is they never get caught."

"There's no hold on this generation of kids." Patterson grimaced as they rode up the elevator to their desks.

"That comes from single parents, TV, and a lack of old-fashioned whooping."

The elevator stopped on their floor. They walked to their desks, passing a few officers who eyed them keenly. A female officer pulled Blondie to her desk. Blondie looked to the other officer, then turned to Patterson.

"Go on, I'll meet you upstairs in five minutes."

As Patterson walked off, Blondie's friend Kelly looked him over.

"Why didn't you tell me your new partner was so handsome?" she whispered.

"He is, but I'm not paid enough to go around telling every female that works here. Correction, every *single* female."

Kelly looked Blondie up and down, waiting for an answer.

"So, I guess you want me to put in a good word?" Blondie asked.

"Or I'll think a married woman is tampering with official goods."

"Oh, no." Blondie looked at Kelly with an evil smirk. "You wouldn't."

"Oh yes, I would." Kelly grinned in return.

Comment on her mind, Blondie walked away from Kelly's desk without looking back. She knew if she didn't hook Kelly up, her name would be station gossip for the next month or so.

Upstairs in the profile room, she sat, one hand going through her hair as the other turned the massive pages in the mug shot photo album. Patterson walked over with two cups of coffee, handing her one.

"What's with the dried-out face? Did your friend say something bad?"

Taking a sip, she leaned back in her chair and looked at him, Kelly's musings sticking with her.

Damn, he's handsome. Those piercing eyes dig right into my soul.

"Blondie." Patterson waved his cup from side to side in her face, bringing her back to reality. "Are you worried about something?"

"Well, kinda. It's today's shooting. A little girl was taken to the hospital, and she was safely in her house."

"Damn. How is she?"

"She's stable, but Detective Mullens says it was done by my guys."

"How could it? We left them around the same time the shooting took place."

"No… We saw them approximately an hour before."

Sitting back, Patterson crossed his legs and rubbed his chin. "So it's a possibility it could be them."

"I know it's them. And that Kevin is involved somehow."

"Calm down. Don't go accusing with your feelings."

"I'm not accusing! I know!"

"Tell you what. Let's go to the pub and have a drink. On me."

"I don't think Kelly would like that."

"Well, if she finds out, tell her I'll be drilled before I go out with her."

Blondie got up from her seat and walked over to the coffee machine. She stood there, thinking about being alone with Patterson, and quickly shook her head. She wondered where those thoughts had come from. Turning back, she made a quick decision.

"I'm sorry, but I can't. I have to go home and patch things up with my deadbeat husband."

"I bet you'd feel better listening to him after a stiff shot of vodka to smooth your nerves."

She smiled at his remark. "Well, when I think about it, that might be helpful."

"I'll meet you downstairs. And your friend has walked by the door at least a dozen times, if you haven't noticed."

"Oh," she said with a devilish smile on her face. "She's waiting for my signal."

CHAPTER SEVEN

The evening of Chris's first day on the job, a day he wouldn't forget, came and went. And it all began with killing somebody for the second time in his life.

He sat quietly in the car as he remembered the dilemma.

He heard the fat guy at the table tell the big guy to shoot him, but with quick thinking, he somehow managed to get the gun out of the thug's hand and turn it on him.

Flashbacks of his first murder came hurtling into his mind. Despite being clean, his hands felt hot and slick as if blood coated his palms.

"Is you alright, Chris?"

Not looking Reggie in the eye, Chris replied, "Yeah. It's not like I haven't done it before."

"Get over it. We're a team now, me and you, and we got things to do, places to see, and people to meet."

"What a way to start the first day, huh?"

Reggie smiled, and they drove off.

For the rest of the day, Reggie took Chris to all of the private and local hot shot clubs, underground gambling joints, and pimp lairs.

As the night grew dark, they took refuge at Reggie's most frequented and favorite night club. A unique setup, the front entrance resembled a barber shop. Then, a small hallway led to the entire club.

As Reggie walked in, everyone greeted him—a toast, a slap on the shoulder, female waitresses even kissing him on the cheek. They took a seat in the far corner of the room. There, Chris sat in silence, observing the happenings.

A sultry waitress with nearly nothing on came over to their table. Chris's eyes widened as he took notice of her large bosom and hairy crotch, inches from his face.

"Hi, Reggie," she said. "Haven't seen you in a while. What's been going on?"

"I've given up on the night life."

"Don't tell me you've finally found a real woman."

"You got that right, Lips. I'm getting married."

"Lips?" Chris butted in.

Looking back and forth between them, Reggie smiled.

"I think you better show him why they call you Lips!"

"Come with me, honey. Any friend of Reggie's is a friend of mine." Lips pulled Chris out of his seat as Reggie pushed him up.

"Go on, she won't bite," Reggie pressed.

Chris had no choice. Lips led him back to a room with only a bed in the middle. Before he could say a word, he was backed up against the wall, dick out of his pants. With those cherry-red lips around it, he was too busy climbing the walls of ecstasy to speak.

Back at the table, a few friends visited Reggie to find out what went down between him and Carlos. They laughed and chatted. After a few minutes of gabbing, he saw Chris limping as he returned to the table.

As he sat down, Reggie whispered, "She's something else, isn't she?" in his ear.

"Uh-huh."

"I used to limp the same way, but since I met your sister, I haven't been back until today."

"I don't think I have any dick left."

"Is that good or bad?"

Smiling at him, Chris glanced around and changed the subject.

"Why did we come here in the first place?"

"To meet Mae-Lyn. She's the one who deals with everything."

"A woman runs this dump?"

"Not only this dump, but the goods, too, now that Carlos is gone."

"You think she knows?"

"Yeah. She knows everything. Maybe she'll reward you. But let me tell you, she's a real bitch."

"If that's the case, I don't want to meet her."

"I don't care as long as we break bread with Mae-Lyn. Oh!" Looking at the front door, Reggie noted a flurry of movement. "Here she comes now."

A heavyset black woman walked in surrounded by three large men in suits. Clad in furs and a lot of jewelry, she contrasted with the petite black girl who travelled behind the entourage, the total opposite of her aunt. Chris wondered why she was with a crowd like them. The scene didn't suit her. Mae-Lyn was escorted over to Reggie's table. Everyone except Reggie and Chris got up, clearing the space. The two ladies sat down.

"Can I get you something to drink?" Reggie asked, gesturing to the bar at the other end of the club.

"No, thanks. I heard what you did to Carlos."

"Straight to the point. Same old Mae-Lyn. It was ruled as self-defense."

"You don't have to explain shit to me. I never liked him in the first place."

"Thanks. That takes a lot off my head. By the way, this is my brother-in-law."

"I already know. He just got out of juvenile prison."

"This woman don't miss a beat," Chris noted.

"Chill out, kid… So, Mae-Lyn, what's the deal?"

She turned to her niece and said, "Why don't you two excuse yourselves. I'll send for you when I'm done."

The niece got up without even glancing at Chris and headed for the outside yard. Chris slowly followed. There, they sat away from each other. Occasionally, each would catch the other's glance.

"Aren't you scared of going back to prison?" she asked, breaking the silence.

"Why? Once you've been there, the rest is easy. Besides, we did the police a favor."

"My father liked Carlos."

"Why did you come here? This doesn't look like your kind of setup."

"My aunt usually has me tag along. Something about the family business that I must learn."

"You don't seem interested."

"I'm not. I hate violence, drugs, and men hounding me like I'm a piece of meat."

"You're beautiful and powerful."

She smiled at his remark. "And you're not the mobster type, either."

"I wasn't until today."

"I can tell. You look surprised at everything."

"I'll be even more surprised if you go out with me."

"Are you hounding?"

"Far from it."

"What movies do you like?" she asked.

"I'll let you choose. That'll add to the surprise."

One of the bodyguards came to the doorway, motioning to the two. Mae-Lyn's niece got up to leave, then looked back in Chris's direction.

"By the way, my name's Lyn."

"Mine's Chris."

Inside at the table, Mae-Lyn got up to leave.

Before handing him a piece of paper, she said to Reggie, "Remember, I'm your friend, but my brother isn't, and he wasn't pleased to hear that Carlos is dead."

***

On their way back to Reggie's house, he handed Chris a piece of paper. He looked at it, raising an eyebrow.

"What's this for?"

"That's one option: kill or be killed."

"Huh?"

"Remember what I told you? Mae-Lyn knows everything. Her brother doesn't take lightly to Carlos being killed."

"I thought you said she's in charge?" Chris asked.

"Yeah, but her brother is the shot-caller, and he wants us dead. The only one on our side is Mae-Lyn, and right now, there's a choice. Kill her brother, or get killed."

"You sure it's not a setup?"

"I don't think so. She's not too much in favor of her brother, either."

"Damn... the shit people do for money."

"She's been waiting for this chance. We're just stuck in the middle." Reggie shook his head.

***

Sitting in a booth at the pub sipping on strong shots of vodka wasn't like Blondie, but between a hectic day and a nagging husband to go home to, it seemed the best thing to do. Especially when it left her sitting across from a handsome man and just talking, something she hadn't done in a while.

Patterson reached across the table and gently rubbed her hands. She jumped, looking at him, then smiled.

"I saw you go off for a minute. I had to bring you back."

"Thanks. It's been a long time."

"Since you had a clear conscience?"

"Don't tease me."

"Well, it's my first day, and I still don't know my partner."

"What is it you want to know?"

"For one, you daydream a lot, and that interests me."

Perhaps it was the vodka loosening her tongue, but she sat up and cleared her throat. "Well, I've been married six years. No kids. I'm from a little town called Clarkville in Idaho. My age doesn't matter right now… and I'd like to think I'm easy to get along with."

"What about your love life? Not that I want to get too personal."

"I see you get straight to the point."

"I'm sorry. You don't have to answer. It's just that I can't picture a man not being overjoyed with your presence, much less being married to you."

"Thanks for the compliment, but it's more than that."

Patterson thought about changing the discussion as Blondie sulked down in her seat, but she kept going.

"The problem is he doesn't approve of my job. I like my job, and for the past few months, we've been fighting and seeing less and less of each other. Now, he spends more time with his business than with me."

"Did you guys try talking to a counselor?"

"It's no use. He hates shrinks."

"So, what's next?"

"Divorce." She twirled her ring as she spoke, her voice affectionate and soft.

"I think the two of you should sit down and try to save your marriage."

"Jesus, please," she scoffed, tossing back the rest of her drink. "You don't know the half of what I've tried. Jacob's just… He's so *stubborn*."

"I can imagine."

"Enough about me. Let's hear your story."

"Well, mine is quick. I was born in New York. My parents died in a car accident when I was twelve. I moved to D.C. with my aunt and uncle, went to school, and then the Academy. I've never had a love interest, and now I'm here."

"I'm sorry to hear about your parents."

"That's alright. I'm over it, thanks to my aunt."

Blondie looked at her watch, took one last sip, then sighed. "I'm sorry, but I should be going. I enjoyed your company. Thanks for everything."

"No. Thank you."

She got up and walked off. He watched her leave, taking his glass between both hands and rolling it from side to side. Leaning back in his seat, he closed his eyes.

***

On the highway back to the hood, the two cars raced each other to see who would get back first. Mike and Fat Al were in one car, Corey, Pee-Wee, and Stokey in the other.

"Drop me off first," Stokey said. "I'm going to surprise my girl."

"Why didn't you ride with Mike?"

"I'm not getting in no car with Al-man."

"Keep on fucking with that girl, and she's gonna fuck you over one day," said Corey.

"You need to get a life. Let me do this."

"Why don't you be like us? Fuck 'em and duck 'em," Pee-Wee suggested.

"I don't go around sticking my dick everywhere—"

"Oh, shit! Look, Corey!" cried Pee-Wee. "It's your mom!"

"Damn! What's she up to now?"

He sped up, then cut across the street. Car horns were blowing every which way. Ignoring them, he swerved onto the sidewalk.

"You better get her some help before she embarrasses you in public," stated Pee-Wee. "We deal, but we gotta keep our families outta that shit."

"Man, shut up! I told her to get into one of those rehabs."

"Why would she? Her son has a cure right at home."

With that comment, Corey stomped on the brakes. The other two collided with each other, nearly hitting the windshield.

Corey was the first one out of the car, followed by the others. They were still rubbing their necks as they ran into an alley.

At first, there was no sign of Corey's mother, but knowing the type of lifestyle she was into, it wasn't hard to locate which direction she'd headed. After all, at the end of the alley sat an abandoned house where the neighborhood crackfiends congregated.

Corey didn't wait for an introduction. He ran straight into the house to find his mother. The other two stood outside in case of trouble.

Inside, the house was dark, musty, and reeked of crack. With the help of some sunlight coming through a hole in the window, Corey's eyes adjusted to his surroundings as he searched. She wasn't downstairs, so he ventured upstairs, where he caught sight of her loading a crackpipe.

He ran over and snatched her up. Pearl fought against his pull, and other fiends got up in her defense. Thinking quickly, he reached for something under his shirt.

He backed up, then threw the crack and pipe down. The fiends immediately forgot about the situation and hurriedly attended to finding what was thrown. Corey then took ahold of his mother and dragged her down the steps and out of the house. She trembled and cried as he walked her to the car, the others following in silence.

Ten minutes later, they arrived in front of his house. His mother was the first one out, running inside.

She slammed the front door in fury.

"It's hush-hush with us," Pee-Wee assured Corey.

"I'm gonna stroll on down to my car. See you freaks later," Stokey said, waving as he dismissed himself. The other two went back into the house, Corey walking up the stairs to his mother's room as Pee-Wee hung out in the living room downstairs.

Inside, she was crying. As she saw Corey, she ran and hugged him.

"I'm sorry, honey. I didn't expect to see you."

"Mom, you've got to get some help. Sooner or later, the whole neighborhood is gonna find out."

"All I wanted was one hit."

"Look, Mom." Pushing her off, he looked directly into her eyes. "I'm not going to supply your habit any longer." He turned and walked out the door, wiping tears from his eyes as he headed down the stairs. He partially blamed himself for his mother's sorry state, and it had to end.

Pee-Wee jumped up from his place on the couch as Corey entered the room.

"She all right, man?"

"I guess so… Let's go."

"You sure you still wanna go? Maybe you should hang around."

"You and I both know that you can't tame a crackhead."

"What? Man, that's your mother."

"So is all the ladies we sell shit to. Why don't you feel sorry for them?"

"But…"

"Man, shut up. Come on, let's just leave."

***

Back over at Kia's house, Steve was doing what he knew best: putting in some steamy lovemaking between the sheets. Rolling out of the bed and onto the floor, he picked her up and headed for the living room, then started all over again. Finishing up, they sat together, legs tangled on the couch.

Steve spoke first. "How could you worry about me running around if I'm bedding you like that every day?"

"It was the best, but that's beside the point. I still don't trust you."

"You got nothin' to worry 'bout, baby," Steve lied easily.

"I just can't believe you. Where were you last night?"

"Missin' you. That's why I came over early today."

"You came over early, alright, but it wasn't for me."

Ignoring her, he reached for the ashtray, picking up a half-smoked blunt and lighting it. As Kia moved away from him, he grabbed her and blew smoke in her face.

"Come on, Steve. Cut it out."

"You got something against weed?"

"You smoke too much."

"What do you call what you do?"

"I never said nothing about smoking, it's just you do it too much."

"They say weed enhances your sex drive."

"Too much of anything isn't good for you."

"Except sex."

Kia got up, stark naked, and walked to the kitchen. She came back with two glasses and a champagne bottle. Sitting back, she filled both glasses and gave one to Steve.

"You ever think about marriage, boo?" she asked as she cuddled up beside Steve.

"What's this, a proposal? I thought that was my line."

"Do you?" she pressed, sipping her drink and looking him straight in the eye.

"Well… I'm not ready, if that's what you want to hear."

"That means you don't love me like you say you do."

"Don't try to trap me."

"What's that supposed to mean?"

"Not that trap. I mean, you know what I'm into. In the long run, you'll end up getting hurt, and I'll be dead or locked up for life."

"Then quit! I love you, and only you. Not your money or your lifestyle."

"If your government didn't look at me as less than a man, I wouldn't be doing the shit that I do."

"That's a lame excuse."

"Oh, is it? I'll bet that I can go downtown tomorrow, apply for seven or eight openings, and never get a call back."

Kia moved closer. She had him right where she wanted him. "I've got a job for you."

"I'm not going to any McDonalds. I'm bigger than that. I should own one, not work in one."

"Calm down, baby. Who said anything about McDs? It's about children."

"You know I can't babysit."

"It's about you teaching! Telling them it's not cool to sell, use, or harbor negativity in their community."

"Listen to what you're saying! I'm not no role model or counselor."

"But you know about the subject firsthand. Who else better than you to give it to them?"

"But…"

"Be at my job tomorrow around lunch time. The seminar starts at one."

Before he could say another word, she started kissing and rubbing his manhood. He flipped her over, and for the rest of the night, they made endless love.

CHAPTER EIGHT

The evening wind picked up. The neighborhood was dead to a certain degree; most people decided to stay in once the sun set. A few passersby roamed the hood, including Mike and Fat Al.

They lurched close to the alley in case robbers or police made a last-minute round. Besides, business was picking up in spite of the weather, and their customers were sticking in the shadows of the buildings to stay out of the wind.

Coming up behind them, unnoticed, was Kevin. He hollered before coming too close, just in case they decided to shoot first and ask who it was later. Luckily, they recognized his voice.

"Hey, why is y'all trying to take my customers?" Kevin asked.

"This fool's trying to make enough money to buy a car tomorrow," Mike said, jerking his thumb at Fat Al.

"Not in one night, he won't."

"I've got some already saved up," Al butted in. "All I need is two more thousand."

"Well, make it fifteen hundred, 'cause I need five hundred. I'm going over to my aunt's house for a while."

"That'll be a smart move," replied Mike, "'cause that bitch wants you bad."

"I'm not stunting that bitch." Kevin walked off to tend to another customer, then came back. "Let's go up to the house. It's too dead out here. The po-po can see us from blocks away."

They wandered off toward the infamous crack house. A few minutes up the block, they saw a car slowly turning the corner.

They didn't wait for an introduction. Kevin pulled his gun as the window of the car rolled down.

"Yo, chill," a familiar voice yelled out. "It's me, Dre."

Fat-Al spoke up with an agitated, "Yo, man! Don't be pulling up like that!"

"Calm down, youngins. You looking for Corey?"

"Nah, and we ain't seen him."

"When you do, tell him I'm at Stacey's."

Dre's window wound back up, and he drove off.

The boys watched his car 'til it was out of sight. They didn't want any last-minute surprises; Big Dre wasn't one of their favorite people. Many plans had been made to rob him and blow his head off, but due to his relationship to Corey, he was spared.

"I hate that dude! He thinks he's the shit. If it wasn't for Corey, we should've robbed him and put them dumb-dumbs in his ass."

"Let's get him anyway. Him and Corey isn't *that* tight," replied Kevin.

***

That night, Chris spent the night with Reggie, struggling to find Big Rich and his bodyguard. Mae-Lyn never told them precisely where to look, but they picked up chatter on the streets.

Quietly creeping down a massive hallway, they stopped at the sound of a toilet flushing. They saw a light come on, then off. A figure came out, then went back to his room.

Little did he know, he was being watched.

Reggie whispered to Chris, and he took off quietly down the hall. He came up to the door the person had gone in. He slowly opened it. Within seconds, flashes of light appeared and were gone. Reggie snuck up beside him, pointing across the hall.

Standing on either side of the door, Reggie eased it open with his foot. As they caught sight of the bed, they both opened fire without checking to see if Big Rich was there or not.

They exited the room, ran down the steps, and left the same way they came in.

They sprinted down the pathway and along the hedges, only to be surprised by what seemed like the whole damn Fairfax Police force. Chris was so surprised that he pissed on himself. Reggie, on the other hand, always thought he'd eventually be taken down during a hit, so he just held his hands up as the floodlights glared into their faces.

All they could do was cringe at the thought of what would happen next.

***

Still on death row, Chris explained the outcome of that hit to the chaplain:

The judge sentenced Reggie to life in prison without parole, and I got twelve years of hard time with no family support. My brother told me I was possessed, and my mother refused to speak to me anymore. Carol still hates me to this day.

At the time of my release, I had nowhere to go, so I called up a buddy of mine named Bull who I met while I was in doing time.

Bull was what a real convict would look like: a cross between Zeus and Kamala, the wrestler. He stayed in the southeastern part of D.C. in section eight housing.

When I arrived at his apartment, I wasn't surprised to see the neighborhood was run-down. It was drug-infested and gutter-ridden, just the way he liked it.

Finding his apartment was like a jigsaw puzzle. As I knocked on the door, I saw the cruddy hallway, and I knew there was more shit going on in there than on the street.

***

The door finally opened, and Chris was greeted with open arms by Bull.

"Hey, looka here! Did they release you, or did ya escape?" he joked as they hugged each other.

"Man, cut the shit." Chris walked in, and, after giving the place the once look over, he chuckled. "Nice dump. I love it. Not to mention your neighbors."

"Better than prison any day."

"Shit must be running slow for you, huh?"

Bull grabbed two beers from the refrigerator, tossing Chris one before responding.

"Fuck, after my last appointment with my P.O., a niggah has to watch his doings."

"So I came at the right time, huh?" Chris asked.

"Don't get too excited. Shit ain't the same no more."

"Fuck your P.O.! We was born to crime! You and me, baby."

Getting up, Bull walked over to Chris and patted him on the shoulder.

"You right, man. Who needs this dump? It's us against the world, baby!"

***

Pulling up in the small parking lot, Pee-Wee and Corey finally arrived at their big date.

Pee-Wee didn't waste time in getting out and rushing up to knock on the door. A young Toni Braxton look-alike opened it. Seeing she was wearing a see-through negligee, Corey was by Pee-Wee's side in ten seconds flat.

"You must be Pee-Wee," she said, pointing to Corey.

"No." Staring at her erect nipples, he pointed to Pee-Wee. "That's him."

Pee-Wee didn't ask to enter. He walked straight in. Corey, on the other hand, waited until the girl turned so he could get a full view.

"Hi, I'm Kelly," she said, "but everyone calls me Sis." She turned to head upstairs, but before she was totally out of sight, Pee-Wee noticed something.

"Where's Pepsi? She's mad at me, huh?"

"Yeah, she is. She left with Paula to get some more weed. Waiting on you was useless."

"Who else is with her?"

"Some more of her girlfriends." Kelly's voice faded as she disappeared upstairs.

Pee-Wee joined Corey on the couch as he fumbled with the remote. After flicking through various channels, nothing caught their attention.

The kitchen was the next best option. As they walked in, Corey went straight for the refrigerator. There wasn't much inside, though more than the average girl's house.

Looking back at Pee-Wee, he said, "They don't make hookers' houses like they used to."

"Broads is too independent these days."

"Fuck independence. Where's the homely touch? All these chicks keep around nowadays is cosmetics and a box of Arm and Hammer," Corey complained.

"I guess if we ain't there for them, they stray."

"If they acted more like mommas, I'd be there." Corey walked over to the table to make a sandwich.

"I hope Pepsi ain't real mad with me. I'm horny as shit."

"I'm about ready to unload, myself."

"Pass me a plate. I'll roll some joints while you make sandwiches."

Kelly entered the kitchen. Looking at Corey, she smiled, walked over, and sat right on his lap.

"If you act right," she said, "your wish might come true."

"Don't try me, girl."

Pee-Wee pulled him close and whispered in his ear, "Don't move too fast. You might like one of the other ones better."

Kelly reached over Corey and smacked Pee-Wee. "Don't put any ideas in his head." She reached across the table and picked up one of the blunts. Lighting it, she held the smoke for a few minutes, then let it out slowly. Corey began to get a hard-on just watching her chest go in and out.

She felt the rise in his pants and turned around. "Wanna give me a shotgun?"

He didn't need to hear that twice. He knew when a girl asked for a shotgun, she was ready to get twisted.

Pee-Wee couldn't stand the sight of those two at the table, groping and sucking on each other. He got up and left.

A little while longer, and he would've come in his pants.

***

At Stokey's apartment, he and his girl, Taria, were lying back on their love sofa, watching TV. Taria kept fondling his dick and kissing him all over.

"Come on, girl, what's with all the extra energy?"

"'Cause I know you bought me something today."

"Where'd you get that idea?"

"My girlfriend saw you coming out the shops."

"So? That still doesn't mean I bought you anything."

"Well, who else would you go into a diamond store for?" Taria sat up and crossed her arms. "It better not be no other bitch!"

"Damn... I can't surprise you with nothing, huh?"

Getting closer, she rubbed his chest and murmured, "You know I love you, baby, and I'm very jealous of my man."

"Yeah, right... Come here." He picked her up and took her to the bedroom. As the door closed, the front door quietly opened, and a male figure silently stepped out.

***

Back at Pepsi's house, Corey and Pee-Wee were in heaven. While Pee-Wee and Pepsi settled their differences, Corey was having fun, going around the room full of beautiful women. He blew smoke in their faces, dancing to the D.C. beat of go-go music as he sipped on champagne. Everybody was getting twisted, and Corey fit right in.

"I like this, man," he yelled over the music to Pee-Wee. "Maybe we should move in."

"You can if you're willing to pay the rent," said Pepsi.

"No, no. I'll leave that to Pee-Wee."

"That cheap mothafucka? All he's good for is some dick."

"Ain't that enough?" Pee-Wee laughed.

Corey didn't want to get tangled up in the middle of the pair's love-war relationship. He quickly strolled over by the other girls.

Kelly kept a keen eye on him. No matter what it took, she wasn't about to let him slip away with Paula. The other two girls were both dykes, so they weren't a problem, but she wanted to keep an eye on them as they huddled over by the door, passing a joint.

"Hey, what's with the silence?" Corey asked.

"They're too fucked up to say anything," Kelly explained.

Paula, hearing Kelly, whispered something to the girls. Slowly getting up, they walked to the middle of the room and began to strip each other down to nothing but their underwear.

Corey's expression told Kelly to move quickly over by him. He was on the verge of jumping all over the first girl he could get his hands on.

Pepsi got up and dragged Pee-Wee into the bedroom with her. Kelly attempted to do the same with Corey, but he was transfixed by the performance in front of him.

The two girls kept at it, things heating up. They started to go down on each other, sucking, licking, and fondling to the brink of orgasm.

Kelly didn't have to persuade Corey any further because he had turned to her and was stripping her down to nothing. She obliged by returning the favor.

Paula, amused by the amount of power a woman had over a man, felt left out. So she went over to join the two girls.

***

While Pee-Wee and Corey enjoyed themselves in the company of too much pussy, Fat Al, Mike, and Kevin hung out, smoking a blunt at the crack house.

Someone knocked at the door. Mike got up and looked through the peephole as the other two took positions in case of a robbery. Turning around and letting them know that it was okay, Mike let Fat Al move to the door while Kevin stayed on the stairs with his gun out.

Fat Al saw who it was and eased the tension. "Oh, that's my man, Heavy. I've got what you need, baby! Big ones." He held out a hand filled with rock cocaine.

"Let me get this," Kevin hollered from the stairs. "All I have is five joints left."

"You don't know how much he's looking for... How much you want?" Al asked Heavy.

"I need six."

"Gimme one of yours, Al," said Kevin.

"Is it the same, Al?" Heavy asked.

"Yeah, we got the same shit. Here."

Fat Al gave Kevin one of his, Kevin made the transaction, and the crackhead left. As Heavy walked out the door, Kevin handed Fat Al a twenty-dollar bill.

"Don't surprise me by pulling out some more shit," Fat Al grunted. "I told you what I'm trying to do."

"Chill out, man. That's it."

"Yo," Mike interrupted, "what you gonna do about that bitch, Blondie? You know she's out to get you."

"I know. I want to catch that bitch so I can blast her." He emphasized his point by rattling the gun in his hand.

Fat Al shook his head, counting his money.

"Yo, this shit's a trip," he said to no one in particular. "We make all this money in a few hours, while regular people break their backs doing this shit legit."

"It's a helluva feeling being your own boss, huh?" replied Kevin.

"We'll never be that. Imagine us doing somethin' legit with this money! The feds would find a way to take it back," replied Fat Al.

"Come on, man, don't say that. There's plenty of ways to clean up bad money. Don't you be watching them mafia movies? You see how they do it," answered Mike.

"They're white. Whites look after each other," Kevin stated.

"So what you're saying is that a black man ain't got shit coming in America, huh?" asked Fat Al.

"Unless he's an Oreo cookie," Mike laughed.

"What?" the other two asked in unison.

"You know… white on the inside, black on the outside."

A knock on the door interrupted their conversation, and everybody took their positions. This time, Fat Al answered the door. He made another transaction, then returned, picking up the conversation where they left off.

"So, Mike, what you're saying is I can't be rich in America unless the white man works me to death first?"

"You see what they're doing? First, they gave us the drugs thinking all we was gonna do was use them; now we flipping the script, taking 'em, and building legit."

"I say we make enough, then get out. That way they can't tie us to nothing dirty," Kevin suggested.

"That's you. I don't trust the government. I'm living mine up," replied Fat Al.

"That's why we can't get nowhere with niggahs like you in the game."

"Say what you want. It's my money."

"I'm about to beep Rasta. Let's smoke some of 'em with Kevin since he'll be gone for a while," Mike suggested, changing the subject.

"Why don't you get some juice while you're down there?" Fat Al asked, giving him some more money.

There was another knock, and since Mike was on his way out, he checked before opening the door.

Two ladies waited outside. He opened the door and let them in, walking past them as he headed out. They sat down on the couch, eyeing Fat Al and Kevin expectantly.

"We're broke and we need a hit," one of them said. "Is anyone trying to go?"

Fat Al looked at Kevin. When he didn't get an answer, he turned to the ladies and said, "I'm ready, but my buddy's a virgin. He's scared of pussy."

"So what about me?" the second lady whined.

"If she does a good job, I'll call you up next."

Laughing to himself, Kevin shook his head. "You is one freaky mothafucka."

Fat Al ignored Kevin's remarks as he led the lady up the stairs past him. He stopped at the top, turning and throwing him a plastic bag filled with rock-cocaine. "What else is there to do but make money and freak out?"

The other female got up and moved toward the door. She turned to Kevin and said, "I'll be back. I left my cigarettes in the car."

Kevin didn't pay her any mind as she walked out.

On her way to the car, she noticed the police parked in the alley. She ran back to the house, slamming the door behind her.

"There's a police car in the alley with nobody in it!" she squealed.

Kevin raced up the stairs, banging on the door.

"Yo man," he yelled, "the feds are outside! Let's go!"

Fat Al didn't have to hear that twice. He was out the door and down the steps right behind Kevin, who led the way to the back of the house. At the back door, he stopped so suddenly that Fat Al ran right into him. Kevin peeped out, looked up and down the back alley, then immediately took off straight across Jo-Jo's back yard.

He knocked on the basement door.

As Jo-Jo let them in, the crack house behind them was raided with full force.

Outside, Mike walked up with the juices, waiting to see his friends come out in handcuffs. But when only the ladies surfaced, he was sure they had left. After waiting a few more minutes, he headed down the block.

He knew exactly where to find them.

On the corner of the block, Jo-Jo stood with the rest of the spectators, wondering what all the commotion was about. Mike walked slowly past, nodding in his direction to catch his eye.

Down in Jo-Jo's basement, the three boys enjoyed their smoke and sodas while the heat cleared up outside. After a while, Jo-Jo came downstairs to check up on them.

"Hey, Joe! They still out there?"

"Yeah. They're questioning those females."

"Here, man, go smoke this. Good looking out." Fat Al handed Jo-Jo some rocks, then headed back up the stairs.

***

That night, Chris and Bull sat around smoking and drinking, smiling at Chris's proposal.

"How long has this been on your mind, man?" Bull asked with a chuckle.

"I had the inside scoop from some old-timers back in the joint."

"Man… shit ain't the same."

"I know. All I'm doing is perfecting it."

"Cut the shit! An armored truck scene? No way."

"It's either all the way, or no way at all."

"It's likely to get pretty bloody, but what the fuck! Shit happens, huh?"

Slapping each other high fives, Chris mentioned, "One more thing… It's gonna be downtown, right under their noses."

They pulled out another beer and toasted to their plans.

The next morning, they checked into a motel right across the street from the First National Bank. Outside, a dozen money trucks lined up. Since the one they wanted arrived at noon, they sat and watched patiently from their window.

***

Fat Al, Mike, and Kevin came out of Jo-Jo's house at about seven a.m. Skeptical, they stood on the porch and scanned the street before they decided to leave.

Walking down the block, Fat Al nudged Kevin's ribs.

"Hey, Kevin? Just to remind you, you owe me a hundred dollars."

"A hundred?! For what?"

"I saw you throw my shit to that broad."

"You damn right! I wasn't about to get caught with your shit!"

Mike pulled out some weed, unwilling to listen to them go back and forth. They both fell silent as he passed it to Al.

"Hey, slim..." Al said to Kevin, "you know Blondie's coming out early today."

"Let me get something to eat first, then I'll catch a cab."

"I'd love to eat *that*," Mike cut in, pointing across the street to a beautiful white girl.

"A white woman? Man, you need a checkup," replied Fat Al.

"What's wrong with white broads? Pussy is pussy."

"What's wrong with black pussy? Are you scared of them 'cause they're too aggressive?"

"Now you trying to start somethin'. I never mentioned anything about not wanting a sister."

"You live in a black neighborhood, and here you are lusting after some white meat!"

"They do give good head," interrupted Kevin.

"Black girls do too!" replied Fat Al.

"I ain't trying to hear it. I just want to hit it," said Mike.

"Now I see why you ain't got no girl. Them Playboys keeping you busy, and now all you see is white women."

"I think she's mixed." Kevin smiled, watching her pass. "Look at her ass!"

As they walked past her, she caught Mike's stare as he winked at her. She blushed as they went into the store.

CHAPTER NINE

Steve stood in Kia's kitchen, getting something out of the refrigerator. He didn't notice her creeping up behind him until it was too late, and she caught him in a hug from behind. He turned slowly and kissed her.

"Did you think about what I said last night?" she asked.

"I was too busy doing other things to remember," he murmured, grabbing her cheeks.

"No, seriously. I'll tell my boss you're willing to help."

"I'll come if you promise never to bring up anything about me being a no-good boyfriend."

"Cross my heart."

"Look, I'm about to leave. Call me when you get to work."

Giving her one last kiss, he grabbed his coat and left the house.

In the car, he checked his beeper to see if anyone had called. Starting the car, he noticed an unfamiliar number. He reached for his cell in the glove compartment and dialed the number as he took off down the street. It rang a couple of times, then someone picked up.

"Hello?"

"Who's this?"

"It's Audrey. Is this Steve?"

"Audrey who?"

"Jesus… From the McDonalds, boy!"

"Oh! What's up? It took you long enough to call."

"I've been calling all night! Ever since I got off work."

"Couldn't get me off your mind, huh?"

"Don't push it. You still want a challenge? I'll give you one!" she teased.

"What brings you to that conclusion?"

"Oh, just wondering."

"What'cha doing later today? Trying to go to lunch?" Steve asked.

"I did a double shift. I really don't want to leave the house."

"Can I come by and massage your feet?"

"I don't know… You might try something."

"Only the feet. I promise."

"Where are you at?"

"I just left my grandmother's. She had me cutting grass all day, so I stayed over."

"Bet."

He drove through Corey's neighborhood. Passing his house, he decided to stop.

As he got out of his car, he noticed the front door was open. Not receiving any answer when he knocked, he went up the stairs. Seeing Pearl's bedroom door was open, he peeped in to see if she was there.

Lying on the floor in a fetal position, she was soaking in a pool of blood.

He stood there for a second, paralyzed and unable to move. It took him a while before he could pick up the phone and call the police.

Within a few minutes, an ambulance showed up. Behind it came the cops, and with them was Blondie.

She met Steve at the steps after the detectives had taken a few statements.

"Well, Steve, how are you gonna tell Corey about this?"

"Me? That's your job. All I'm gonna do is get him."

"I saw a bunch of your buddies on Taylor Street while I was coming up. Knowing them, they might be on Upshur Street by now, though."

"Thanks for the support, Blondie. I'll holler."

"Oh, by the way, tell Kevin I'm gonna get him. Even if it's the last thing I do!"

"Yeah? You tell him when you see him."

He didn't look back as he walked off.

Down on the block, everyone was present except Kevin. Messing with girls, selling drugs, and gambling, they were doing what they did best.

Steve slowly pulled up. As he got out of his car, he saw Corey running over to Big Dre's vehicle.

"Hey, Steve!" Fat Al greeted him, walking over. "That thing must've been really good last night, huh?"

"Regular... pussy, dick-suck."

Hearing the conversation, Pee-Wee butted in, "Shit, me and Corey was getting fucked while two more broads munched on each other."

"Stop lying! Y'all ain't got it that good," replied Steve.

"Yeah? Wait till Corey comes over here. You can ask him yourself."

"Hey y'all, speaking of pussy, I think I want to marry my girl. Who'll be my best man?" Stokey interjected.

"Nobody! We don't like the broad!" yelled Mike.

"I don't care. That's my pussy."

"Don't talk too fast. She's only fucking with you until she finds out where you keep your stash. Then, that so-called cousin of hers is gonna come and get it," said Al.

"Yo, Steve!" called Mike. "There's a new girl in the hood, and I think I want that!"

"You forgot to tell him about the white part!" replied Fat Al.

"A white bitch, huh?"

"I guess you don't approve either, huh?"

"Not really. I just want to know if I could hit it sometime."

"Depends."

"On what?"

"If she's like what I've read in books, you can't have her."

"There you go, housing the pussy before even getting it." Fat Al laughed.

"She's got a black body with a cute white face. She's similar to Mariah Carey."

"Mariah ain't white." Steve shook his head.

"Tell the white folks, not me."

"Fuck the bitch, I got five on a fifty bag!" Stokey cut in.

"You cheap motherfucker, you can put up more than that!" replied Fat Al.

"I'm the one buying the shit! My car, my gas."

"I'll put three dollars to the blunts," Mike offered.

"There goes another one…"

Walking back from across the street, Corey shook his head, complaining to no one in particular. "That niggah is jive! Putting the press on me about his money? Somebody loan me two G's."

"Fuck that punk! I don't know why you still deal with him," answered Stokey.

Steve walked over to Corey.

"Let me talk to you for a minute," he said, motioning away from the group. Corey nodded, and they walked off down the block.

"Hey, man, you got two G's I can borrow?" Corey asked.

"Nah, man. Check this out… I stopped by your house a few minutes ago, and… I found your mother dead on the floor."

"What?!" Corey grabbed Steve as his knees went out.

Steve tried to help him up, but his weight only got heavier. The other guys saw what happened and ran toward them.

"Everything all right?" Al asked, concerned.

While Corey was crying in his arms, Steve told the others what he'd found, sparing the details where he could.

Everyone stood around Corey in silence, listening as he mumbled to himself between sobs.

"It's my fault," he whispered to Steve. "It's all my fault…"

Leaving their normal evening activities, the guys all went up to Corey's house to support him.

***

It was five minutes before twelve. Chris and Bull stood across the street from the bank and watched as the noon crowd grew thicker and thicker. They checked their watches.

It was time.

The money truck pulled up, and the two took a look at each other. After this, there was no turning back.

The guards came out of the truck, opened the back door, and began unloading. A tourist bus pulled up behind them. As the door opened, a bunch of kids piled out.

While unplanned, it was perfect timing.

The two men walked silently across the street, barely noticed by the surrounding people. Before the guards sensed what was happening, Chris and Bull pulled up on the two in the rear. A third officer from the bank came out to light a cigarette, saw the assault, and immediately pulled his pistol.

He fired, hitting Bull in the arm. Chris returned fire, knocking the officer down.

The sound of gunshots sent everyone into a panic, running, screaming, and ducking for cover. A few kids stood in shock, unsure of what to do in all of the commotion.

Chris ran away with what he had in his hands, blending in with the crowd. Bull slid under a car and went for the alley.

In minutes, the bank was surrounded by the entire police force, but by that time, Chris and Bull were long gone.

Six hours later, Bull was being treated by a nurse who lived in his building while Chris watched. She didn't ask why Bull got shot. She knew anything was possible in their neighborhood. After she left, the men looked at each other and smiled.

A few months later, they were living it up, investing in cars, girls, and a lucrative drug business. As far as they were concerned, they were on the top. The world belonged to them.

One particular day, Bull and Chris visited their count house. It was run by a longtime friend of theirs named Scuba. She was a hard woman, taking no shit from anyone, including them. They liked that about her.

Lounging inside her pad, she placed two cans of beer in front of them.

"Look, motherfuckers!" she blurted out. "All ya pay me to do is collect and count, plus make sure nobody gets ripped off."

"So? What is you getting at?" replied Bull.

"What I'm saying is I'm not your maid! Next time, get the beer yourself."

"But we didn't ask you to get us any beer."

"You was getting ready to." She stood in front of them, pointing her finger as she accused them.

Patting her on the behind, Chris chuckled. "Don't mind her. She's probably on her period today."

"I'll be on your ass in a minute if you don't shut up."

"Yes, ma'am… So, how did we do this week?"

"Can't you read?" She threw a piece of paper at them. "It's right there in front of your face."

"Sixty thousand? Hell, no! Come on, Scuba, stop playing!"

"I'm not playing. Most of the shit was bad, and that makes for bad business. Whoever you got this shit from, they got over." She took a seat beside Chris.

"Let me see the phone," Chris said. "I'm about to find out." He dialed his man Fast Eddie and didn't waste time getting to the point.

"Yo, Eddie, what's up? This last order is fucked up, man!"

"Yo, don't blame me! Ask Charlie. He's the producer. I just sell the shit."

"Tell him to call me. I'm at Scuba's house."

"What did he say? We getting our money back?" Bull called from the kitchen as Chris hung up.

Scuba cut in. "What y'all need to do is quit this shit and go legit. This drug game is played out. Hell, you got enough money."

"You might be right, Scuba. But remember? We've got records. We can't go legit."

"Find a way. This game don't last forever."

"The game never changes," replied Bull. "Only the players."

"Don't fool yourself. The government ain't putting up with this shit for too long," answered Scuba.

"I don't see why, if it's their shit," stated Bull.

"Talking like a true niggah in a black man's world."

"What's that supposed to mean, Scuba?"

"You know the truth, but you riding with the enemy."

"If it wasn't for drugs, your ass'd be on welfare." Bull laughed.

"You the one with no education. I've got skills, baby."

"I've got skills too! Work for the government, then turn around and sell it to their kids."

"That's why they're locking all you niggahs up and throwing away the key."

The conversation stopped as the phone rang. Bull reached for it.

"Hello, Rockefeller Center. What's up?"

"This is Charlie. I heard what happened."

"I know you did. We want our money back."

"You'll get it back. Y'all ain't the only ones complaining."

"How long, slim?"

"Some new shit in today. I'll call you back."

"We should stop doing business with your country ass."

"Come on now, take it easy. Tell you what, I'm having a party tonight. Y'all come down and relax a little."

"Where'll it be at?"

"Ramada Inn on Twelfth Street. See ya there. Bye-bye."

***

Back at Corey's house, everyone gathered around to show support. The last of the police were still asking Corey questions after telling them that his mother had slit her wrists and bled to death. And after reading the note she'd left him, he felt even more responsible.

Eventually, the questions ended, and the detectives allowed Corey to go about his business. As he walked into the living room, he looked around at all of his friends' sour faces.

"I don't know why y'all're feeling sad. I'm the one without a mother."

"Shit, I know how it feels," said Mike. "You forgot that I lost my mother too."

"What did the feds say, Corey?" Stokey butted in before any sort of argument started.

"After the autopsy, I have to call my aunt. She'll know what to do about the other stuff."

"So, what happens in the meantime?" asked Fat Al.

"I say we chill with Corey," Steve suggested.

In solidarity, they ordered pizza, and everybody stayed the night with Corey.

***

Corey's mother's funeral was a small but sincere service. All the boys went, and afterward, they sat around on the block, drinking and smoking weed all day.

That night, at Corey's house, he suggested, "Let's get out of here."

"Where do you have in mind?" Steve asked.

"Anywhere other than this house."

"I say Atlantic City," Fat Al suggested.

"Your freak ass would come up with some shit like that," stated Mike.

"That's fine by me," said Corey.

Without hesitation, they left straight for Atlantic City.

***

The same evening, at Blondie's house, she and her husband sat on the back porch, talking and enjoying some champagne. Jacob toasted her.

"You know, honey, it's a shame we don't do this more often. You're always off chasing bad guys, and I'm piled up with extensive contracts, hoping I don't come home one day and…"

"Knock it off, Jacob. Why can't we enjoy a wonderful evening without you bringing up what I do?"

"Because I love you, and I care!"

"Oh, bullshit! If you cared, you'd stop breathing down my neck and respect what I do."

"I do respect it." He turned toward her. "But I'd feel happier knowing you don't have your life on the line, or that you could get killed any day!"

"Well, guess what?" she growled, springing up out of her chair and glaring at him. "Tough luck. Either you live with it, or you don't!" Without another word, she walked into the house, slamming the door behind her.

"You'll thank me one day, honey!"

She grabbed her keys and coat, went out through the front door, got in her car, and drove away.

***

Before hitting the I-95 North to Atlantic City, the guys pulled up at their favorite weed corner. Mike jumped out of his car and offered to go get the smoke.

"Hey," Steve shouted out of his ride, "get a quarter pound. That should last us."

Mike took off down the alley. It was dark and eerie to non-weedheads, but to people like Mike, it was the perfect spot. As he walked up to The Basement—as that particular house was called—he bumped into someone he thought would never be caught in that type of place.

"Damn! Watch where you're going!" said Mike.

"Excuse me?!"

"Hey... hold on. Aren't you the same broad that just moved around my way?"

"Since when you owned something?"

"Don't get smart with me. Come here."

"I've got to go. I'm late." And she left without saying another word.

Mike got what he came for, then went back to the car.

"Yo, man! That white chick I told ya about was in the spot getting some weed!"

"You want to hit that, huh?" Fat Al chuckled.

"Yeah!" Mike grinned. "I like her ass!"

"Well, catch her on the rebound. Let's go!" They hopped back in their rides and continued on to their destination.

***

That night at the party, Bull, Chris, and Scuba were greeted at the door by Charlie and two females. They hugged, shook hands, and walked in.

Inside, the party was jumping with high rollers, pimps, and hustlers. Everybody who was somebody was there, and Bull was living for the exposure. After getting a table, he tapped Chris on the arm.

"It's a good thing we came, huh? It's full of important people! We might get lucky!"

"It's full of a bunch of motherfuckers who need to get their lives together!" Scuba butted in.

"Who asked for your opinion?"

"Chill out, y'all. Just enjoy yourselves," Chris said with a smile on his face.

A few minutes went by, and Charlie walked over to their table.

"Is everything going smoothly, guys?"

"Nope." Bull chuckled. "I want to fuck the best thing you've got here!"

"That'll be hard to pick. They're all pros." Charlie called two beautiful ladies to stand by him and said, "Would you like both, or will one be fine?"

"I'll take them, and the one who just walked in." Bull pointed to a familiar face only Chris knew.

"Now"—Charlie turned to Bull—"that's probably the hardest thing to get here tonight."

"And why is that, Charlie?"

"Because she owns the damn hotel and everybody in it."

"Well, well… if it isn't Mae-Lyn's niece!" Chris murmured.

Bull chimed in, "You know her, Chris?"

"Better than you think. It's been a long time."

"And what's that supposed to mean?" Charlie asked, watching a mean look spread across Chris's face as memories resurfaced.

"Her aunt's the bitch," Chris said slowly, "that got me twelve motherfucking years!"

"That's her niece, huh? Didn't you tell me that you almost had her?"

"Yeah, almost."

"This is interesting. Maybe I should start a reunion?"

"Shut up, Charlie. I'll reunion myself!"

Chris got up and walked over to where she was sitting. As he slid up to her, she looked at him, speechless.

"Don't look so surprised. I want to kill your aunt, not you." He picked up her drink and swirled it in the glass, taking a sip. "Where is she, anyway?"

Lyn tried her hardest to speak, the words coming out one by one.

"She's a vegetable right now, but if you insist, she's at the Brewster Memorial Hospital."

"Shit, that's the best news I've heard in twelve years!"

She kept staring straight into his eyes, watching him in a show of mixed distrust. He moved closer to her, and she edged away. Her friends had no idea what that man was doing there.

Lyn finally decided to break the ice, asking, "So… are you still in the same business?"

"Not really, other than wanting to pay your aunt back."

"The word around is you and your new partner are swinging it big time."

"You haven't changed, huh? Still know everything, but not involved."

"I'm not in the business. I just know people who talk."

"So, since Mae-Lyn's out of the picture, not to mention your father, who's in charge?"

"It sure as hell's not you!"

"I was thinking we should pick up where we left off twelve years ago."

"Picking up where we left off might be dangerous for the both of us!" Lyn said, getting up from her seat and disappearing into the crowd.

***

Blondie spent the night in a hotel. She tried to sleep but couldn't. Sitting up in bed, she looked over at the clock, watching it blink 2:40 a.m. back at her. Time slid past. She must have had too much to drink; all she recalled was driving from one corner of the district to the other.

Then her husband came to mind, and she remembered who had caused her to be there that night. She reached for the phone as a hot wave of guilt rolled over her, but she thought against it and headed out the door instead.

Twenty-five minutes later, she pulled up in front of her house. She entered from the side door, just in case her husband was waiting up for her. Taking her shoes off, she tiptoed up to her bedroom and opened the bedroom door.

Stark naked on the bed, the maid was riding Blondie's husband cowboy style.

They were really into it. Several seconds passed before they realized she was standing there. Her husband knocked the maid off one side of the bed as Blondie turned for the door and ran down the stairs.

As she reached the front door and flung it open, she was confronted with another nightmare staring her right in the face.

Kevin had an automatic weapon pointed right at her. But, hearing the rumbling as Jacob made his way down the steps behind her, he looked over her shoulder for a second.

That was all the time she needed.

She jumped to the side at the same time Kevin opened fire. Her husband didn't know what hit him.

From behind her, Blondie heard the two German Shepherds snarling and racing toward the front door. Kevin shouted incoherently, and she heard his yells fade into the night as the dogs tailed him.

Crawling on the floor, Blondie reached for the phone. Only after dialing 9-1-1 did she look down at her leg and realize she had been shot.

Within minutes, Patterson and some other officers were at her house. She was taken to the nearest hospital, and Patterson rode with her the whole way.

***

It was early in the morning when the guys finally arrived back from Atlantic City. The small trip had been good for Corey, and they all gathered around in front of his house when it was all said and done, smoking and sipping on whatever they had left.

A car pulled around the corner, heading in their direction. Mike reached into his glove compartment and pulled out a gun, only to stop as a familiar voice came screaming from the other car.

"Don't shoot! It's me, Puffy!"

Mike put the gun back in his waist as the car pulled up closer.

Pee-Wee didn't give him a chance to introduce the other girls in his car. He hopped inside, hands all over them.

"I told ya this was gonna happen," Puffy said to them, turning around in his seat.

"Get out of the car, and stop scaring them," Stokey grumbled at Pee-Wee.

"I hope one of them is like Puffy," said Al.

"What you saying? My type isn't just as good?" Puffy asked.

"Yeah, it might even be better! But not with us."

"What the hell you doing out this early in the morning, anyhow?" asked Steve.

"We coming from this party. Them guys was all over me and stuff. I had to leave before they tried to rape me!" said Puffy.

"Yeah... or put one in you and then left your ass for dead when they found out you's a man!" Steve said.

"Oh, stop talking dirty to me! You make me think you want some!"

"When is you bringing us some more clothes to buy?" asked Mike.

"Darling, I'll bring you anything for your cute self."

"Yo, Puff!" Pee-Wee yelled from the back of the car. "Her right there is not leaving! She's coming home with me!"

"No, I'm not!" replied the girl.

"You is if I say so. These my peeps," said Puffy.

"Fuck it, leave them all here! I need somebody to cheer my man up," agreed Steve.

"I was wondering why he was so quiet, knowing him to be a freak." Puffy chuckled.

"His mom died. He hasn't been himself lately." Steve pointed over to Corey, who was sitting on his steps.

"Hey, Shameeka, come here!" Puffy called over one of the girls from his car, who got out and walked over to him.

"Look, girl, go over to him, and don't leave until his dick falls off. Then, give me a call."

Puffy turned to the rest and asked, "Other than Pee-Wee, anyone want to choose before I leave?"

"We straight. Take Pee-Wee with you."

"Corey, take care of my girl."

"Sure will."

Satisfied, Puffy got back into his car and pulled off with Pee-Wee in the back.

Steve turned to Corey and asked, "You straight for the night? 'Cause I'm heading in."

"Yeah." Corey pointed at Shameeka. "I am now."

"I'm gone, too," Stokey butted in. "I know my girl is mad at me for leaving and not telling her."

"If she was worried about you, she would have beeped you," said Al. "And she ain't going to."

"You're a pussy. Just drop me off on the block."

"That's all you do with your time, huh? Spending it in the crack houses?"

"What else? I'm trying to get paid. The hoes come later."

"I'm gonna get me some weed and turn in," said Mike.

Everyone jumped in their cars and went their separate ways.

CHAPTER TEN

The night went well. Chris and Bull got their drugs back, plus two new ladies to take home. They had everything they could possibly want.

Well, almost everything.

Lyn had turned Chris down, something he wasn't accustomed to. Even with the last smart remark she made, he couldn't stop thinking about her. So he decided to take action. Chris made it his business to find out where she was staying.

With a few connections on the street, he came across an address. He sent all kinds of roses and dinner invitations.

She turned every one of them down.

One day, while hanging out at the barber shop, a kid ran up to him and gave him a letter. Bull looked over at him from the other barber chair, wondering what it was about. As Chris opened the note and read it, a big smile crossed his face. He ran out of the shop without saying a word to anyone.

Within minutes, he was parked in front of the old movie theater on Fourth Street. In front of it, Lyn stood waiting for him. As he got out of his car, he felt like he was moving in slow motion, caught in her beauty.

By approaching her, it was as if he'd stepped on sacred ground, but when he finally gathered his courage to speak, she put a finger over his lips.

"Let's just finish the date first."

He nodded, holding her hand as they walked into the movie theater.

Later that evening, as they stood in front of his car, he asked her what made her change her mind.

"Well, the word around was you were doing everything in your power to find me."

"It had to be more than that."

"Also, I figured if you still carried any hatred, it wasn't for me."

"That's the past. Let's keep it that way."

They kissed, then got in their cars and drove off.

As the months rolled on, they saw more and more of each other, and Bull began to suspect that his iron-hearted buddy was falling in love.

One night, at the local bar, Chris finally decided to tell Bull something he'd been thinking on for a while.

"Man, I'm quitting. You can have the business. Give me my half, and you can do whatever you want with the rest."

"What?! You can't cop out! You started this. I'll be nothing without you!"

"I'm my own boss. If I want to quit, that's my choice."

"The dogs won't like this, man."

"That's just too fucking bad, man!"

"It's that girl, huh? What the hell do you see in her? She's bad news, man, just like her aunt."

"Oh, shut up! She's not in the game. She knows nothing like this."

"I'm not gonna be around you with that negative talk, man."

Chris left his partner without saying another word.

He pulled up at Lyn's house. After blowing the horn twice, she came to the door, surprised to see him come around. He jumped out of his car and ran to her.

"Get your things, baby. We're going to celebrate!"

"Celebrate what?"

Pushing her toward the house, he said, "Just get your clothes and meet me in the car."

They spent the rest of the day cooped up, occupying each other at Chris's apartment. Too into each other to go on into town, one thing led to another, and they ended up in bed, making the best of a romantic evening.

The next morning, Lyn rolled away from Chris, kicking off the sheets that tangled her legs. She got up quietly, walked in the kitchen, and made breakfast.

Moments later, Chris crept up behind her. She jumped at his touch, then relaxed as he started to kiss and caress her neck.

"Oh, that feels good!"

"You sure it won't get in the way of your cooking?"

"Only if it goes up a notch."

She didn't need to tell Chris a second time.

The next thing she knew, they were on the kitchen floor. They migrated to the living room, then back to the bedroom.

When the phone rang, neither of them wanted to answer it. After a few repeated attempts, however, Chris finally decided to pick up.

"Hello, no one home."

"Cut the bullshit. This is Dog."

Sitting up, Chris replied, "Didn't you get my message? I'm out!"

"Not until we talk. Meet me at the restaurant at twelve o'clock."

"Alright, fine!" Slamming the phone on the receiver, he turned to Lyn and picked up where they'd left off.

"Is everything okay, Chris?"

"Better than I expected."

She recharged his erotic senses with a hug and a kiss, and they were at it again.

Twelve o'clock came too quickly for Chris. It seemed as if he was just getting started with Lyn. While she lay there asleep, he jumped out of bed, showered, and left.

Before entering the restaurant, he noticed Bull and the Dog were already seated, Dog speaking on the phone.

***

"Look, don't worry about the death of your father. It'll be repaid. I promise you."

"That motherfucker better be dead by two o'clock!"

"Trust me. I've got an even better plan."

"Better than a bullet in the head?"

"Lyn, I'm hurting too. Just let me handle this."

"No fuck ups. Bye."

***

Chris walked into the restaurant, waved at them, and walked over. "What's up, fellas? Let's make this quick."

"Check it, slim. Since I wasn't aware of your departure, you're obligated to one more ride," said Dog.

"Hell, no! I quit!"

"This is the last one, and it's big. You can take it all or split it with old Bull here."

"What are you, deaf?"

"Three hundred thousand. Take it or leave it!"

"Three hundred thousand? What? What the hell is he talking about?"

"Before you announced you were splitting off," Bull butted in, "I took a lot of smack from Dog. Now the stuff's here, and he wants his money."

"Let me put it to you this way: I *need* my money. You're half in with Bull. Either help or suffer. And you know how I like to make people suffer!"

***

Still at Chris's apartment, Lyn picked up the phone, dialed, then spoke.

"They're all there. Make it quick and clean!" She returned the receiver to its rocker, then repeated the process.

"Hello, 9-1-1? There's an emergency at 1200 Pennsylvania Avenue. Hurry!"

***

Back at the restaurant, Chris checked his watch. He didn't plan on being so long.

"Your half is right here," Dog continued. He pulled out a briefcase from under the table. "Take it or leave it. Either way, I want my money."

Chris took a cigarette from his pocket. The two men watched as he got up, walked out the front door, and leaned against the wall outside. While puffing away, thinking about Lyn and how he was going to pull the hustle off, he looked up and down the avenue. He noticed several cars were identical. Too many. The restaurant wasn't packed, either. And the cars weren't there when he'd pulled up. He threw the cigarette down and walked quickly back inside.

"Yo!" he yelled at the other two, sprinting up to the table. "This place is crawling with cops!"

"Yeah? Tell them I said to come in for a drink!" said Bull.

Bull didn't get a chance to finish laughing before the front door was kicked in. He reached for the briefcase, but Dog was quicker. He grabbed it and headed for the back door while the police checked everyone to be sure it was safe.

One of the officers, however, noticed the three men leaving through the back.

"Hey, you! Stop!"

They ignored him, moving through the restaurant and trying to find an exit. They were greeted with gunfire.

"Damn! What the hell is this?" cried Dog.

Everyone headed back the way they'd come: through the doors, and right into the arms of the police.

Bull pulled out his gun and looked at Chris. "I'm not going back to jail, man!"

He fired at the cops, bullets flying back and forth. During the exchange, two rounds hit Bull in the chest. Confused, Chris looked around and around, trying to find someone to help his buddy who was bleeding all over the floor.

The ambulance eventually arrived, but Bull was dead minutes after he was shot. Chris and Dog were charged with possession of the drugs. Chris got eighteen years, and Dog walked away with probation.

Chris's whole life caved in, just as he thought he had beaten the system.

One day, while in jail, he was called for a visit. Lyn had finally come to see him.

"Hi, Chris. Why didn't you bother to call?"

"For what? I'm broke. I've got too much time to do. I don't need any extra problems."

"Well, guess what? You have a big one, and I'm *carrying* it!"

"Don't gimme that shit! If it was mine, it wouldn't have taken you so long to tell me!"

"I was seriously considering losing it."

"So why didn't you?"

"That's for me to know, and for you to find out."

"Whatever, lady. See you in eighteen years."

"If you even live that long." She got up and left, leaving him stunned.

A few years went by, and a kid who was down with Dog was booked into the prison. Another inmate pointed him out to Chris, and he approached him on the yard.

"Yo kid," he hollered, "you one of Dog's boys?"

"Who wants to know?"

"An old friend of his. My name's Chris."

"You ain't that Chris he talks about at the restaurant shootout?"

"Yeah, that's me. Did he mention that he still owes me money?"

"Nope. The word is he wanted you dead that night, but the cops ruined it."

"I figured something was funny."

"It had to do with an old debt he needed to fulfill."

"Is that right?"

"Yeah. That's why I'm here. I was supposed to clean up a job for him."

"He's still using people, huh?"

"Not really. This lady was using him. He's kinda scared of her, so he wanted her out."

"A woman? It's not like Dog to let some skirt run him off."

"Her family's powerful. She's the one who set up the restaurant job to wipe you out. Now, Dog thinks she might do the same thing to him."

"Huh… huh. I wonder who wanted me dead that bad?"

The two men took a seat on one of the yard benches, Chris silent as he stared up at the sky.

***

After getting his weed, Mike made one last round of the neighborhood. As he drove up Taylor Street, he noticed a figure walking a couple blocks up.

As he passed the crack house, he saw Fat Al sitting on the steps. He honked his horn and kept going.

The figure he saw turned out to be the white girl he'd run into at the weed spot. His imagination started to get the best of him as he pulled up beside her.

"Yo!" he shouted out the car window. "I see you're working the graveyard shift too, huh?"

"Excuse me?"

"Where you coming from this time of morning?"

"None of your damn business!"

"It is when you're prowling my neighborhood."

She stopped in her tracks. "You don't own shit, and it's my business what I do, coming or going."

He jumped out and walked over to her before answering. "I really don't care what you do, but I do care if you end up getting hurt. This hood can get real nasty at times, even for cute snow bunnies like yourself."

"It's good to know that people with your line of work are considerate of others."

"Hold on, now. What the hell are you talking about?"

"I know about you and your friends. You don't think it's a secret, do you?"

"So what? I sell drugs. What that got to do with love?"

"Love? Who said anything about love?"

"You don't have to say it. It's written all over your face! I can see you dig me."

"Maybe. But not with you sneaking up on me, demanding to know where I've been."

"I'm not sneaking! We do this every night. Makes sure there's no surprises."

"So, is you gonna take me home, or are we gonna stand here until people start coming out to go to work?"

"You don't have to tell me twice."

***

Back at the crack house, Fat Al took a break and relaxed on the steps. With a bag full of twenties on his lap and a gun in his hand, he was getting sleepy, nodding in and out.

Two cars pulled up. Al jolted and sat upright as a crackhead approached him and bought three twenties before walking back to his car.

Another pair came to him next: a man and a girl who looked too beautiful to be smoking.

Fat Al's eyes lit up. As they approached the steps, he put the gun to the side and started to fumble with the bag.

In that moment, two men hidden between the cars opened fire on the group.

All three got hit. Fat Al and the man died instantly, while the girl was still breathing when the ambulance finally showed up.

***

Pee-Wee returned to the car he'd left by Corey's house. Piss-drunk, he kissed the girl he had forced himself upon, then kissed Puffy before staggering out and making his way to the car.

Pulling up beside him, Puffy asked if he'd be alright to drive.

"I'm... just getting... my shit."

"Okay. I'll come by to check on you tomorrow."

"Sure... bye."

As they drove off, Pee-Wee sat behind the wheel. He looked at Corey's house, then at his car keys. After several minutes of deliberation, he finally decided to drive off to nowhere in particular.

A few minutes later, he stopped at the corner of Georgia Avenue and Columbia Road. At the light, he saw a girl getting pushed out of a car. He pulled up beside her and gestured for her to get in.

"Which way you heading, sweets?"

"Nowhere in particular," she said, hopping in. "I just had a fight with my boyfriend."

"I can see that… So, you trying to hang out?"

"I don't care."

Driving off to his favorite hideout, he continued with the conversation.

"So, what made ya get into it? You catch him with another girl?"

"I told him I wanted a real man. He took it the wrong way."

"Shit. Since he don't trust you, I might as well be the man."

"Come on, you just met me!"

"As pretty as you is, I'll be a real anything. I'm going to a hotel. You can sleep in your clothes if you want to."

She didn't answer, and Pee-Wee grew more sure of himself, getting ready for what would go down after they got there.

***

Stokey opened the door to his apartment, then quietly tiptoed to the bedroom. The light inside told him his girl was still up. He even heard music playing. It wasn't like her to get romantic without him. Maybe she didn't know he was coming.

But on the other hand, she knew everything. He smiled and gently pushed the door open.

At the sight in front of him, his knees buckled. His mouth opened, and his jaw moved, but he couldn't utter a single word.

In front of him, on his bed, three people were enjoying their erotic passions. Two of the three were giving, while the one in the middle was receiving both ways.

They were too far into their performance to notice him standing in the doorway.

"Taria!"

All three of them jumped up as if their mother had caught them, and Stokey finally found his voice and screamed. Without giving them a chance, he reached into his jacket pocket and pulled out his gun. He commenced firing and didn't stop, even after he was out of bullets.

Moments later, he stood over the bloody mess he'd made. Up one wall and down the other, dark red and brown mingled, soaking into the fibers of the bed and carpet. The three bodies were almost indistinguishable from one another as they slumped together in a fleshy pile.

By the time the sound of sirens brought him back to his senses, he knew it was too late. He went to the front stoop of the building and sat on the steps with the still-smoking gun in his hand.

***

In the hospital, Blondie was treated for a graze on her leg. She was out in no time and was given a few days off, considering what had happened to her.

When she gave her report on the assault, she told them she didn't see her attacker's face. While it was just a little lie, she couldn't give up her shot at Kevin. This time, she knew it was to be either him or her. But one thing was for sure; in their next run-in, one of them was going to die.

Her husband's funeral was nothing but a formality for Blondie. Patterson was there to comfort her, but she couldn't even bring herself to fake a tear as Jacob's body was lowered into the ground. Instead, she glared at the crying maid who had the guts to show up at all. But that evening, while Blondie and Patterson were drinking coffee, the conversation turned to work.

"So… it was Kevin, wasn't it?" Patterson asked.

"Kevin, what?"

"Don't play dumb with me. You could be thrown off the force, or worse, put in jail!"

"Look, whatever I do is my decision, okay?" She got up and walked to the window without even looking at him. Tears rolled down her cheeks. "That little fucker took two people out of my life. He has it coming!"

Shifting the conversation, Patterson decided not to push her. He'd get back around to it before it was too late.

"You know Fat Al got shot, and Stokey is at the jail for wiping out his girl and two guys?"

"Say what?"

"Yup. It seems like everyone in your hood is coming down with a case of bad luck."

***

At ten forty-five, the lunch bell rang. The kids from the junior high and high schools flocked to the neighborhood stores, getting their usual cheeseburgers and fries, fish sandwiches, and chicken-wing specials from the Chinese store. The park was filled with everyone doing their own thing.

Cars flew up and down the street in circles, hoping to catch them a freak, whether it be a boy or girl. Young hustlers came by in new rides, trying to catch the eyes of young girls, most of whom got tricked, fucked, then dumped by three o'clock.

While the everyday activities took place, a group of boys kept to themselves on Upshur Street, disturbed by the news they'd received about their friends. Pee-Wee, Corey, Steve, and Mike sat on one of the neighbor's steps, discussing what had gone down.

"I'm kinda fucked up… I wasn't there for Fat Al," said Mike.

"It's not your fault, man," Steve replied. "Shit happens."

"I say it's them bammers! We should go blast their ass!"

"You can't say that. It could have been some other crackheads."

"I don't buy that. The police found his drugs. Crackheads wouldn't leave that lying around."

"Corey's right. It just might've been them niggahs."

"Stokey called me," Steve mentioned. "We got to go see him."

"Over at the jail? Man, it's bad luck to go over there. Next thing you know, we'll be joining him!" cried Pee-Wee.

"If it was you, we would've been there since last night," Steve argued.

"Yeah… you right. But first, we gotta stop by the hospital."

"For what? Don't tell me you're burning again."

"I say we drop him off at Upper Cardoza. Nobody would recognize him," said Mike.

"Fuck you, Mike! I said the hospital, not see-it-all, tell-it-all."

"Why don't you wear condoms, man?"

"They make my dick feel small in that shit!"

"Like you ain't trying, huh?" laughed Corey.

"It ain't his dick. It's them big-pussy hoes he be falling in love with," said Mike.

"It ain't funny, Pee-Wee. You gonna catch that shit one of these days, and then you'll really be fucked up!" Steve warned.

"Niggah, don't bring that AIDS shit to me. I ain't catch it yet, so I'm never gonna get it."

"Yeah? It's never too late!"

They all got up, jumped in Steve's car, and drove off.

First stop was the children's hospital. Inside, they amused themselves by checking out the beautiful nurses while Pee-Wee filled out all of the necessary paperwork.

A nurse walked up to the bunch and asked, "Which one of you gentlemen is here to see the doctor?"

"Him!" Mike pointed at Pee-Wee. "He's on fire!"

Everyone but Pee-Wee found Mike funny, and he glowered at them as he handed her the clipboard.

"So," the nurse replied, "I imagine the rest of you is clean?"

"Clean as a whistle, miss," Mike said, mocking the nurse's tone of voice.

"Have any of you taken an AIDS test?"

"We don't have to. We wear condoms, and plenty of 'em," Steve said.

"So, it wouldn't hurt if we took one, right?" Corey suggested.

They looked at the nurse, then each other.

Pee-Wee was called into a room.

"Yo!" Mike shouted after him. "Take that test while you're getting plugged, too!"

"So, what's up? It's not gonna hurt, plus we can have any girl we want," Steve pondered out loud.

"Fuck, yeah! We just flash the paper saying 'negative,' and the broad won't think twice," Corey agreed.

"What if she flashes hers after you fuck her, and it says positive?" Mike laughed.

"Then I'll kill the bitch!"

The guys walked over to the nurse's desk, got the necessary papers, and filled them out. They followed the nurse one by one into a room for their tests. When it was Steve's turn, he sat in front of her, arms stretched out.

"Yo, nurse, how long before we know what's what?"

"It'll come to you in the mail. That is, if you live somewhere."

Outside, they waited on Pee-Wee to come out. As he met up with them, he raised an eyebrow.

"The nurse told me ya took an AIDS test, too."

"Yeah, to get that shit out of our system," replied Mike.

"Yo, nurse! If my shit comes back negative, will you go out with me?" asked Corey.

"Sorry. I don't date thugs."

"Yeah? You better start. The only real men left is us!"

"Is that so?"

"Here's my number. Hit me one late night when your man's scared to come pick you up."

They left and headed for the jail to see Stokey. Outside, they pulled up into the parking lot. It was a trip to see a hospital on the same lot as the jail. There, the only place a black man landed was either his deathbed or locked up for life.

It wasn't a good day; the jail was packed with visitors, the line winding all the way outside and around the corner. They decided to wait in the car until Steve and Corey saw a familiar face. They shared a smile.

"Look," Corey said, "that broad in the coat with tassels, that's the one Steve put out of his car and left the bitch out on the road."

"No! I did no such thing!"

"For real, man. He's a dirty dude."

"Damn! She's real healthy in the ass area!" said Mike.

"She looks healthy everywhere," replied Pee-Wee.

"Go get her, Mike! Let's see your work!"

"Naw, I'm alright."

"Don't tell me that white girl got you pussy-whipped!"

"Hell, no! I'm just alright. Let Pee-Wee get her."

"I can't. My game's too vicious. She's gonna want the dick right now!"

"Both of ya some shit," said Steve. "Come on, let's try to get in. We might have to pay someone."

They all got out and walked over to the entrance. The girl saw Steve and Corey, then turned up her nose at them. They laughed as they passed her. However, when they found the inside was even more hectic than the outside, they decided to wait.

***

They weren't the only ones waiting. Back in the hood, Kevin was waiting for Big Dre to exit a store.

Dre came out with a bag and walked over to his car. Kevin waited for the right moment, then jumped out from behind a nearby car, causing Dre to drop his bag. Nobody in the store noticed anything as Kevin pushed his gun into Dre's side and motioned for him to get in.

Once they were in the vehicle, Kevin checked him for a gun, then commanded, "Don't say shit! Just head for your house."

"What's up with this, Kevin? This shit ain't called for."

"Didn't I say shut up, punk?" Kevin smacked him across the face with his gun. "Drive to your house!"

Big Dre started the car and pulled out, leaving his bag still sitting on the ground.

Pulling up, Dre tried to plead one last time, but Kevin didn't wait for words. He popped him in the back of his head, then headed inside, taking the back entrance.

He heard music coming from the kitchen, where he found Dre's girlfriend dancing around as she washed the dishes. He crept up behind her and grabbed her mouth with one hand, holding his gun to her head with the other.

He whispered, "Take me to the money, and you'll live!"

She shook her head, then headed for the living room. Pulling the television set to one side, she picked up the carpet, revealing a loose floorboard.

Kevin walked over her crouched figure and shot her several times. He pushed her to the side, gathered all the money, and left.

***

That night in the pen, Chris was sleeping until a note was dropped off in his cell. He woke up and read it, and a few minutes later, his door was popped. He gathered up his clothes and headed for the showers.

Walking down the aisle, everyone stared at him. Someone passed him a knife. He rolled it into his clothes, stepping into the shower as a few other inmates came out.

In the shower, Dog's lackey-kid came in. He turned on the shower and began lathering, but his soap slipped out of his hands and rolled down the tile. As he grabbed for it, he was stabbed several times in the back before he fell to the floor.

It was a long time before the officers came running, but by then, it was too late.

***

Blondie decided to roam the neighborhood. She knew nobody would expect her to be back so quickly after what had happened. But in a sense, she wasn't. She wasn't in uniform, nor in a police car. That day was personal, and if she wanted something that badly, she had to go out and get it.

Cruising through the neighborhood alleys, she decided to rest a minute. As she reached for her purse, a shadow slipped by. She looked up, only to see a male's back as he walked down the alley.

She didn't pay him too much attention until he pulled a shiny object from his waist. A gun. She didn't panic, picking up her cell phone to call 9-1-1. While waiting for someone to answer, the male figure turned his face so she could make out his identity.

"9-1-1, what is your emergency?"

She only answered, "Wrong number," before hanging up. Watching the figure as he exited the alley, she quickly pulled her gun and got out. She knew, as she ran down the alley, that she had him.

As she rounded the corner, she and Kevin stood face to face.

He fired two quick shots. She fell, shocked and shaking, blood oozing from her mouth. Kevin stood over her, smiling down at her writhing form.

A shot rang out from nowhere.

The expression on Kevin's face changed. His knees buckled, and he fell, landing on top of Blondie.

Behind them, Patterson ran up and stood over them both. He shook his head and walked back to his car.

***

The chaplain sat in his chair, contently listening to Christopher's story.

"So, you see, chaplain, killing that kid over hearsay, plus finding out that my own girl was the one who set me up… Those things build up. But I'm still not satisfied. Why?!"

"*I'm* wondering why someone would have your baby, then want you dead. It makes no sense to me."

"That's where you come in, chaplain. You have to find her. It's my last wish."

"Do you know where she lives now?"

"I have no idea. Her last name's McPherson, if it helps. But I need to hear the whole story from her… face to face."

"Well, let me see what I can do. You know you go up tomorrow. Are you ready?"

"Do I have a choice?"

Heading toward the door, the chaplain paused, took Chris's hands, and placed a rosary in them, then walked off.

***

Coming back from the jail, all four boys were in a daze. Smoking the last of their blunt, they took North Capital, then took a left on Water Street. As they approached the stoplight, at least twenty cop cars flew by, going every which way. They looked on in amazement as the police headed in the same direction they were going.

Steve wanted to turn around but fought the instinct. There were plenty of other blocks with the same negativity as theirs, so there was a chance that it wasn't their spot attracting the police cars.

The boys drove on.

***

Sitting at home, Lyn searched through some old letters. She came upon the one she wanted and slowly opened the envelope. A picture fell out. She picked it up.

It was a picture of Christopher.

The letter inside was from someone else: Scuba. After reading it through, Lyn reached for the phone and dialed the number.

145

***

At least ten blocks up, the neighborhood police cars lined both sides of the street. The hood was at a standstill. Ambulances were everywhere, and roadblocks were set up. The guys pulled over, got out, and walked the rest of the way.

As they approached Taylor Street, Shabby Joe walked over to them.

"Yo, fellas! It's been a helluva bloody day!"

"What the hell you talking about?" asked Corey.

"Big Dre, his girl, Kevin, and Blondie… all dead."

"What the fuck you just say?" snapped Steve.

"Yup! The police are trying to put this shit together now."

"Man, I don't believe this shit! Not Kevin!" Mike shouted.

"Man, let's chill and wait this shit out. They'll tell us without even knowing."

They stepped to the park and sat down to observe the chaos. After about thirty minutes of the police coming and going, putting up yellow tape, and eventually bringing a pair of black bags to the ambulance, the guys left one by one, without a word.

***

That evening, Lyn watched the six o'clock news as she prepared her son's meal.

The lady on the screen brought up the day's murders, stating district homicides were increasing. She talked about the lady cop who was brutally gunned down by a longtime nemesis. The cases of Andrea Cooper, Lynette Davis, and Kevin Sinclair were also said to be tied to the officer who died.

Lyn walked into the den where Steve sat on the couch, talking on the telephone.

"Kevin, Stokey, and Fat Al are gone," she commented. "I guess you'll be next, huh?"

"Mom, that's not nice to say!"

"It's the truth. They say you pick your friends. You know who you are."

"Everybody ain't perfect."

That statement brought back memories. She stood in front of her son, then broke down crying.

"What's wrong, Mom?" Steve jumped up and hugged his mother. "Did I say something?"

"You're right... Everybody ain't perfect." She wiped away her tears and took a deep breath. "There's something I have to tell you. It's about your father and me. Things wasn't perfect between us. That's why we're not together, and why I never talk about him. You see, son..."

The phone rang, interrupting their conversation.

Steve grabbed the receiver. "Yo, who's this?"

"It's me, Kia. Can I come over?"

"Uh, sure. Catch a cab. You'll be just in time to taste my mom's cooking."

Lyn smiled, wiping away a lingering tear. She decided to save the story for another time; she got up and went back to cooking.

CHAPTER ELEVEN

L yn wasn't the only one doing some cooking. Things were heating up at Mike's house as well. He and Jenny had enough water pouring from each of them to boil a cow, as they'd been stirring up some lovemaking ever since Mike left the others at the park. They seemed to be a match made in heaven, unable to get enough of each other.

"Please… time-out…" Mike was almost out of it, pleading with her between gasps. "Gimme five minutes…"

She heard him and stopped for a second, looking up at his face. Then, with a smile, she went back to what she was doing.

"Please, Jenny! You're draining me… I need my strength…" He faded away as Jenny put him to sleep with her efforts to bring his manhood back to life.

While he slept, she sat beside him, looking down on his sweaty face and body and basking in the power women had over men.

***

Corey sat around his living room with nothing special to do. He played with the TV remote and tried not to think about his friends. One day they were all clowning around, and the next… nobody was around.

Is life fair? he asked himself. *First my mother, and now my friends.*

Was there really a God? Did God love what he created, or was Corey's life just amusement for Him? Perhaps it was some kind of specially made project of manifested doom? But if everyone was born to die, was his only true choice whether he'd go fast or slow?

Where was his life going? Was destiny smiling with him or laughing at him?

***

Pee-Wee wasn't the type to just sit around. He was always on the go, and that day was no exception. He felt better moving around than sitting in one place, thinking about all the misfortune happening around him. Frustrated, he headed out of his house and down to the Chinese store to hang out.

A female came out with an older woman who was carrying bags. She saw Pee-Wee leaning on the wall, calling her with his hands, and walked over to him.

"If that's your mother, I ain't trying to get cussed out," he commented.

"Why you say that?"

"That look she got!"

"My mom's always looking at people funny."

"What's your name? I've never seen you around here before."

"I'm from N.E. I've got cousins who live around here."

"You still ain't told me your name."

"You ain't told me yours, either, but mine's Carla. Look, I've got to go. Gimme your number, and I'll call you later." She dug through her purse, taking out a pen and a piece of paper, and wrote down his beeper number. Then, she walked off and got in her mother's car.

Kicking it with the girl didn't satisfy Pee-Wee, however. He still had an urge to do something, but he didn't know what.

***

Steve and Kia lay around in his bedroom, watching TV. She wore one of his T-shirts with nothing underneath, while he was in his boxers.

"Can I ask you something?" she asked.

"Sure. What's up?"

"What will it take for you to quit?"

"Where's all this coming from?"

"Do you need someone else to die or end up in jail?"

"Look, I ain't dying or going to jail, so stop jinxing me." He sat up and turned away from her.

"You can get mad if you want to, but you know the consequences before they happen."

He got up and stormed out of the room, barging straight into his mother's room and lying down on her bed.

He began looking for the remote. Opening the night table, he found it on top of a letter. He noticed that while the letter was addressed to his mother, the sender had his last name. He knew nothing of his father's side of the family. Curious, he opened the letter and began reading.

At that moment, his mother walked in the room and saw what he was looking at. "You couldn't wait for me to tell you?"

"What is this, Mom?"

"That's a letter your father wrote to a friend of his. He don't know where to reach me, so he always writes her, and whenever she talks to him, she lets me know."

"And in return, you tell her you're not trying to be bothered?"

"Well, yes and no. You see, your father murdered your grandfather, and I just couldn't forgive him."

"So, how did I come into the picture?"

"I vowed to do whatever it took to ruin him."

"Does he know me? Or… of me?"

"He knows of you."

"So where does this letter fit in?"

"He's always writing, even though I never answer back. But this time, the lady asked me to call her. She said your father is being put to death soon."

"How soon?"

"Tomorrow. And his last request is to see you."

"Look, Mom, I'm grown. If you're waiting for me to get mad at you or him, I'm not going to. I've outgrown those stages. Whatever ya did, that's your business. If there's anybody for me to grieve over, it's my friends who aren't here with me anymore."

He picked up the letter and left the room. Lyn sat on her bed, surprised by how well Steve had taken everything, then began to cry tears of happiness.

Her son was truly becoming a man.

***

Mike woke up hours later. He felt around the bed for Jenny, but she wasn't there. He lazily sat up, looking around the room. Her clothes were still strewn all over, so he knew she had to be close.

He heard the shower running and slowly walked over to the bathroom to join her. However, hand hovering over the knob, he remembered how carried away she could get and decided against it, heading back to bed for a few minutes.

Jenny's hand reached for the light switch, and she clicked it off. Mike turned over and watched her walk seductively toward him, wearing nothing but the water dripping from her sexy figure. She stopped, smiling at him; then, with a mischievous grin, she jumped all over him.

He flipped her over before she had the chance to pin him between the sheets and held her down. Staring into each other's eyes, they began to kiss. Jenny flipped him back over and repeated the same thing. Looking into her eyes, Mike knew where things were leading, and he decided to change the mood before it got out of control.

"I hope this doesn't stop here, Jenny."

"What do you mean?"

"Love, you know? Black and white... Friends. Family."

"It's the nineties. Who cares?"

"If you really feel that way, fuck it! I can dig it."

***

The next morning, Steve got up without bothering to eat breakfast or speak to his mother. Kia was already in the car waiting for him when he ran out of the house. Getting in, he drove off down the highway.

"Do you really want to go through with this?" Kia asked.

"Why not? I should at least see the man before he goes."

"You're acting like he's just a friend."

"What do you want me to do? Start crying?"

"But—"

"But what? The fucker wasn't there for me, regardless of what my mother did."

"He couldn't do shit. She hates the man."

"I've only heard one side of the story."

They pulled up at the prison, got out, and walked up to the visitor's entrance. Inside, as they waited to be seen, a correctional officer in uniform walked over and offered his services.

"Hello. May I help you with something?"

"Yes. We're here to see a mister Christopher Canine."

"Do you know what section he's in?"

"He's on death row."

"Give me just a minute." The officer walked away, picked up a book, then came back over. He turned through the pages, stopped, then handed the book over to Steve.

Christopher's name was printed in bold letters just under his picture, along with the date and time of death.

"It says twelve o'clock." Steve looked at the officer and asked, "Is it p.m. or a.m.?"

"Keep reading, son."

Steve read on: his father had been put to death by lethal injection at twelve o'clock that morning. Steve's expression changed slightly, and he looked up at the officer.

"Was he family or friend, son?"

"He was my father," he said, getting up.

Kia hugged him as they walked out the door.

"Hey, kid," the officer called after Steve, "would you like a picture of him?"

Without bothering to answer, they turned and walked out the door.

***

The weeks went by, but the tension in the hood didn't change. Ever since Blondie had died, there'd been more police brutality against young black males than gang violence, and yet no one had taken a stand. But life went on.

One morning, the mailman delivered a letter from the hospital to all four boys. Steve opened his and smiled, as did

Corey and Mike. Pee-Wee, on the other hand, didn't seem so happy about what he read. He slowly walked back into his house, closing the door behind him.

That evening, Mike and Steve sat on the wall by the alley, watching the neighborhood kids running by.

"Look, Mike," Steve said. "That's us twenty years ago."

"It's a pity. Look at us now."

"From G.I. Joe to Smith and Wesson."

"Shit, more like poverty, pain, and problems!"

"Look at them. If we don't change, there won't be a future for them."

"Yeah, no bullshit. This shit's like a mirror. Every generation knows the next one's course."

"Yeah, I'll bear witness to that."

THE END

Made in the USA
Middletown, DE
21 September 2023